The Long Chase

Jake Madison was town marshal in Wildern, Wyoming Territory, when his wife Emma was killed during a bank raid by outlaw Bart Peary. Jake quit his job, and embarked on a long chase after the killer.

His pursuit took him to Colorado, the Texas Panhandle, the Indian Territory, and back to Wyoming Territory. In Colorado, Peary, on the run, killed again.

Jake was facing a dangerous and difficult task. Even with the help of a retired Army scout and two elderly prospectors, could he possibly succeed in bringing Bart Peary and his associates to justice?

The Long Chase

Alan Irwin

A Black Horse Western

ROBERT HALE · LONDON

Robert Hale Limited
Clerkenwell House
Clerkenwell Green
London EC1R 0HT

www.halebooks.com

The right of Alan Irwin to be identified as

Typeset by
Derek Doyle & Associates, Shaw Heath
Printed and bound in Great Britain by
Antony Rowe Limited, Wiltshire

ONE

As Marshal Jake Madison and his wife Emma left the doctor's house in the small town of Wildern in Wyoming Territory, they were both feeling that fortune had smiled on them and life could hardly be better. Jake had been given the town marshal's job three years earlier. A big man in his early thirties, square-jawed, and wearing a neat black moustache, he had proved to be a popular and capable law officer. His wife Emma was slim and attractive, with blond hair, a few years younger than her husband.

They had particular reason to be joyful that morning. Doc Kemp had just told them that Emma was pregnant with their first child. They discussed the good news as they went along the boardwalk, then parted company as Jake went into his office. Emma continued on her way towards their house, further along the street. As she was passing the bank on the opposite side of the street she saw the door open and a man standing on the threshold, looking back into the bank. He fired a shot from the six-gun in his hand, then ran towards a horse tied to a nearby hitching rail. The man was masked, and was carrying a canvas bag in his left hand. Emma hesitated, then decided to seek refuge in the general store, which she was just approaching. As she hurried towards the door, it opened and Bob Parton, the deputy marshal, stepped out. He had heard the shot as he was about to leave the store, and he too was holding a six-gun in his hand.

As the masked man reached his horse he saw Parton leaving the store, and fired two hurried shots in his direction. The first shot grazed the side of the deputy's right hand, and he dropped his gun. The second shot hit Emma in the back as she was nearing the door. The masked man mounted his horse and rode off before any attempt could be made to stop him.

The deputy twisted round to pick up his gun. Aghast, he saw Emma holding on to the side of the door, then slowly collapsing on the boardwalk. As he knelt down beside her the storekeeper appeared in the doorway, and both men saw the bullet hole in the back of Emma's dress. Jake arrived a moment later, and knelt down beside his wife. The doctor followed close behind him.

Kemp took a look at Emma. Then he turned to Jake.

'Carry her to my house, Jake,' he said.

Jake picked his wife up and hurried towards the doctor's house, accompanied by Parton and Kemp.

'Get a posse together as soon as you can, Bob,' said Jake to his deputy, 'and follow that rider who just left.'

Parton ran off. Jake carried Emma into the doctor's house and laid her on a covered table. She appeared to be unconscious. Kemp examined the wound.

'It's bad, Jake,' he said. 'First thing is to get that bullet out. And it's not going to be easy.'

With Emma still unconscious, Kemp removed the bullet and cleaned and bandaged the wound. Then, with Jake's help, he laid her in a more comfortable position.

'That's all I can do now, Jake,' he said. 'That bullet's done a lot of damage inside there. All we can do now is wait and see if she comes round. You sit in here with her, and let me know the minute there's any change.'

Deeply worried, Jake sat down beside Emma and held her hand. Over the next three hours she remained motionless, then she stirred and her eyes opened. Instantly, Jake was on his feet, bending over her. She recognized him and tried vainly to speak. Then her eyes closed and her head rolled sideways on the pillow.

Jake called for the doctor, who bent down over Emma for a short while, before straightening up.

'She's gone, Jake,' he said. 'I'm sorry. I did the best I could to save her.'

Jake sat with Emma for a while, trying to come to terms with the sudden tragic loss of a wife and a child. Then he went to the undertaker to arrange for his wife's burial in the cemetery just outside town. Word of his loss had spread, and he received several subdued expressions of sympathy from townspeople.

He went on to the bank, where he found the cashier and the bank manager, whose arm was bandaged. From them he got an account of the raid on the bank. He was told that at a time when there were no customers inside, a masked man holding a six-gun had entered the bank, closing the door behind him, and had turned the notice on the door from OPEN to CLOSED. He then ordered the teller to join the manager who was sitting at a desk back from the counter. He told the manager to open the safe, then stuffed a large number of banknotes into a canvas bag.

The masked man had then backed towards the door. As he half-turned to open it, the manager took a revolver out of the drawer of his desk, intending to fire at the robber as he made his exit. But the move was spotted and the manager was shot in the right arm before he could fire. The masked man had then left.

'I see the doctor's tended to your arm,' said Jake. 'Is it bad?'

'Just a flesh wound,' said the manager. 'Doc says it'll soon heal.'

'I know the man was masked,' said Jake, 'but was there anything about him that might help us to find him if the posse loses him?'

'He was roughly the same build as yourself,' said the manager, 'with black hair and wearing a red shirt. And that's about all I can tell you.'

'One thing I noticed,' said the teller. 'While he was picking banknotes out of the safe, his mask slipped a bit and I saw a knife scar running from just behind his left ear, down towards his neck.'

After getting an estimate from the manager of the amount stolen, Jake left and walked to his office. He was sure that somewhere, sometime, he had seen or heard mention of a scar as described by the teller. Inside his office, he took a sheaf of WANTED posters from a drawer in his desk, and looked at them one by one. Halfway through the pile, he found the one he was looking for. Originating in Colorado, it related to an outlaw called Bart Peary, who was wanted for robbery and murder in Colorado and New Mexico Territory.

According to the poster he sometimes worked alone, sometimes with two or three companions, on bank and stagecoach robberies. Distinguishing features of the outlaw were a scar running down from his left ear, and his habit of wearing a red shirt. Jake was convinced that this was the man who had killed his wife.

The burial of Emma Madison took place the following day. It was attended by practically everyone in Wildern and the surrounding area. When the ceremony was over, Jake returned to his house, still deeply shocked by his loss and the prospect of a future without Emma. Anger welled up inside him as he thought of the callous disregard of the lives of innocent people shown by the man who had shot down his wife.

The posse returned two days later, without the man they had been chasing. Parton, the deputy who had led the posse, told Jake that they had failed to come within sight of their quarry and they were almost certain he had escaped over the border into Colorado.

Jake told the deputy that he strongly suspected that the robber was an outlaw called Bart Peary. He showed Parton the poster.

'This sure looks like the man we were chasing,' said the deputy. 'I got a good look at him before he rode off. What do we do now?'

'I'll send a telegraph message to the sheriff in

Denver,' said Jake, 'telling him that we suspect Peary rode from here into Colorado. I'll ask him to let us know if they pick him up.'

The reply came four days later. It said that there had been only one sighting of Peary, by a homesteader near the New Mexico border, and he was thought to have left Colorado. Jake showed the message to Parton.

'Send a copy of this to the county sheriff,' he said. 'I've already told him about you taking a posse out after Peary. As for myself, I can't rest while this man is still on the loose. I've got to see that he answers to the law for what he's done. I'm going to quit this job and hunt him down.'

'I can understand how you feel,' said Parton. 'Would you like me to come along?'

'I'm obliged for the offer,' said Jake, 'but I want you to take on the marshal's job here. I know you can do it. I'll speak to the town council later today. What I'll do after I've dealt with Peary, I don't know.'

Jake left Wildern the following morning, after handing over to Parton. He had decided to ride to Denver to get from the sheriff there all the available information about Peary.

When he arrived in Denver he soon located the sheriff's office. He found Sheriff Cassidy, a middle-aged competent-looking law officer, inside. He introduced himself. Cassidy rose and shook Jake's hand.

'I heard about your wife,' he said. 'I'm sorry. How can I help?'

'I've quit my job as marshal,' said Jake, 'and I aim to pick up the man who killed my wife. D'you have any information about Peary that might help me to locate him?'

'Nothing comes to mind,' said the sheriff. 'Like we told you over the telegraph, we reckon he's left Colorado and I've no idea where he was heading. But I just had an idea. I took over two years ago from Tom Nelson, when he' retired. Maybe he'll know something I don't. Let's go and see him.'

They found Nelson in his small house along the street. The sheriff introduced Jake, who explained his mission and asked Nelson if he could help.

'I'd sure like to see Peary get what he deserves,' said the ex-sheriff. 'Killing meant nothing to him. But I can think of only one thing that might be useful. I heard tell that his father ran a cattle ranch in the Texas Panhandle, north-east of Amarillo and near a town called Larino. This was about three years ago. The information came from a nephew of mine, Frank Nelson, who runs the livery stable in Larino. Why don't you ride down there and see him? I'll give you a letter for him.'

'That's the only lead I've got so far,' said Jake,

'so I reckon I'll do what you just suggested.'

Jake thanked Nelson, and waited while he wrote the letter. Then he left with the sheriff, who wished him well in his search. The following morning he set off for Larino, which he reached after riding south through Colorado, then across the north-east corner of New Mexico Territory.

Darkness was falling as he rode into town, and the street was almost deserted. He stopped outside the livery stable and walked in. A man was tending to a horse in one of the stalls. He came out to meet Jake. He was a pleasant-faced stocky man, with a slight resemblance to ex-sheriff Nelson in Denver.

'Howdy,' said Jake, and handed over the letter from the liveryman's uncle. Nelson read it, then looked closely at Jake for a moment before he spoke.

'Howdy, Mr Madison,' he said. 'You got a horse out there?'

Jake nodded.

'Well bring it in,' said the liveryman. 'I'll tend to it, then we'll go into the house.'

A little later, in the living room, Jake met Nelson's wife, Mary, who invited him to take supper with them. Over the meal, he told them of his recent talk with the liveryman's uncle, and the reason for his presence in Larino. He asked them to keep this information to themselves.

'You can count on that,' said Nelson. 'About what happened to your wife, we're real sorry. After supper I'll tell you all I know about Bart Peary and his folks.'

Later, as they all sat in the living room, Nelson told Jake that Bart Peary's father, Jed Peary, ran the Rocking P Ranch thirteen miles east of town. The last time Bart Peary had been seen in town was over three years ago, and the story at the time was that he had left the ranch soon after that to seek his fortune elsewhere.

'Has he been back to the ranch since?' asked Jake.

'He could have come and gone without anybody in town knowing,' said Nelson. 'There *was* a home-steader who reckoned he'd seen him near the ranch about three months ago. And that's all I can tell you.'

'It looks like he could be hiding out there between jobs,' said Jake. 'Maybe I can catch up with him here. I'm going to stay around for a while. What sort of operation does Jed Peary run?'

'It's a medium-sized cattle ranch,' Nelson replied. 'He set it up about four years ago, using materials and labour from the south. Nobody from town's been on the place. Casual visitors just ain't welcome. They buy some of their supplies in town but a lot more has been seen coming up to them from the south by freight wagon. Sometimes, we wonder just what's going on there.'

'D'you see Jed Peary and any of his hands in town?' asked Jake. 'That's apart from the hands coming in for supplies for the ranch.'

'Hands come in pretty regular to the store and the saloon,' Nelson replied. 'They're a pretty rough lot, and more of them than you might expect on a ranch of that size. They cause us trouble here. As for Jed Peary, we ain't seen him in town for quite a while.

'Apart from the Rocking P hands we get a lot of strangers calling in, all armed and with the look of criminals about them. We reckon that a lot of them are running from the law and heading for the Indian Territory. Some of them take what they want without paying for it. I can tell you, things have got so bad that most of the townsfolk wish they'd never settled down here in Larino.'

'There's no law around?' asked Jake.

'We get rangers calling in now and again, when they're chasing outlaws,' Nelson replied. 'And that's about all we see of the law. One of the rangers passing through here a few weeks ago on the way back to headquarters told me they'd taken a look at the Rocking P and found nothing suspicious there.'

'I'm going to take a room at the hotel,' said

Jake. 'I'll tell the manager I'm drifting around between jobs, taking a look at the Texas Panhandle. As far as I know, Bart Peary didn't see me in Wildern or any other place, so there shouldn't be any problem about me being recognized.'

Half an hour later, Jake left for the hotel.

TWO

When Jake took a room at the hotel he told Dalton, the owner, that he had ridden up from Fort Worth, taking his time, and exploring the Texas Panhandle. He said that he aimed to stay in Larino for a spell.

The following morning, after breakfast in the hotel dining room, he walked along to the general store. Harvey, a short middle-aged man, was serving two men, each of them carrying a six-gun in a right-hand holster. They glanced at Jake as he came in and stood a little way along the counter, waiting to be served.

When the two men had all the items they wanted the storekeeper totted up the amount owed.

'That comes to two dollars ninety-five,' he said.

Bradley, the taller of the two customers, a big man with a pockmarked face, grinned as he replied:

17

'Now that ain't friendly,' he said. 'We didn't figure you was going to charge us. But if it makes you feel any better, you can have my IOU. We leave in the morning, but maybe we'll be back to pay you one day.'

'I can't run a business like that,' protested the storekeeper. 'For a start, I don't know you.'

'We can soon put that right.' Bradley grinned. 'I'm Smith, and my partner here is Brown.' His tone changed as he continued. 'Make any more fuss about this, and we'll burn the store down before we leave.'

'Pay the bill,' said Jake, turning to face the two men along the counter. His voice was even, but there was no mistaking the fact that he was giving an order. His right hand was touching the holster holding his Colt .45 Peacemaker.

Bradley and his partner, Nolan, turned to face Jake, and stood side by side. Their faces were flushed with anger.

'You just made a big mistake, mister,' said Bradley, 'thinking you could take the two of us. If you want to stay alive, you'll hand over your gun and leave this store right now.'

'Maybe you'd like to try and take it from me,' said Jake.

As Bradley went for his gun, the storekeeper dropped down behind the counter. Just before he disappeared from view he saw the Peacemaker

18

suddenly appear, as if by magic, in Jake's right hand. Bradley made a fast draw, but he was no match for Jake, who sent a bullet into his opponent's right arm before Bradley had time to trigger his own gun.

Nolan drew just after his partner, but Bradley staggered sideways as he was hit, collided with his partner, and Nolan's shot at Jake went wide. Then Jake's second bullet struck Nolan in the right arm. The wound was in almost the same position as the wound on his partner.

Both the wounded men had dropped their guns. Keeping them covered, Jake picked them up and handed them to Harvey, the storekeeper, as he rose into view behind the counter, staring at the two wounded men.

'Hold on to these,' he said, then turned to Bradley, who was holding his wounded arm. As he did so several people came into the store, to investigate the sound of gunfire. They watched as Jake spoke to Bradley.

'That's two dollars ninety-five,' he said.

Cursing, Bradley picked the money out of one of his pockets, using his left hand, and laid it on the counter.

'Is there a doctor in town?' Jake asked the storekeeper.

'Next door to the saloon is where Doc Trump hangs out,' Harvey replied.

'I'll take these two there to get patched up,' said Jake, 'then I'll see that they leave town. Meanwhile, maybe you can find out whether they've robbed anybody else here.'

Harvey said he would do this. Jake took the two men to the doctor's house. He explained the situation to Trump, who took them all inside and tended to the wounds. When he had finished he spoke to the two wounded men.

'You're both lucky,' he said. 'The flesh on the arm is badly torn and the arm is going to be out of action for a while. But it will get better.'

'Luck didn't come into it,' said Jake. 'I wasn't aiming to kill. But these two men are leaving Larino right now, and if they show their faces here again, I won't be aiming for their arms next time.'

Jake saw that the two men paid the doctor, then he took them back to the store, where they handed over the money owed to other businesses in town. He accompanied them while they picked up their belongings at the hotel, and their horses at the livery stable. Then, with Frank Nelson, the liveryman, by his side he watched as they rode out of town.

'From what I've heard,' said Nelson, 'you sure taught those two a lesson. The whole town's talking about it.'

'I'm finding it hard to forget that I ain't a lawman no more,' said Jake.

He went to his room at the hotel and sat on a chair by the window to consider what his next move towards finding Bart Peary should be. He decided that in the near future he would pay a night visit to the Rocking P to try and find out whether his quarry was there. He had a meal in the hotel, returned to his room for a spell, then decided to take a ride through the area around town.

As he approached the livery stable Nelson came out and said that he and the three other members of the town council, who were in the saloon, would like to talk with him. Inside the saloon, they joined the storekeeper, the hotel owner and Ford the blacksmith, who was leader of the council. They all sat at a table away from the bar.

'Mr Madison,' said Ford, 'we have a proposition we'd like you to consider. Folks in town are plumb tired of having to put up with trouble caused by men from the Rocking P and by riders passing through. We sure liked the way you cut those two men in the store down to size. We'd like you to take on the job of town marshal. All we need to know about you is that you ain't wanted by the law.'

'I ain't wanted by the law,' said Jake, then briefly considered the unexpected proposition. He saw that acceptance would provide a valid reason for him staying on in Larino.

'I'll take the job on,' he said, 'with three conditions. Firstly, I can't give you any guarantee about how long I'll stay in the job; secondly, I may have to leave town for a short spell now and again; and thirdly, I would ban the carrying of firearms by any outsiders while in town. They would have to be left at the marshal's office.'

Ford looked at the other members of the council. They nodded their heads.

'Agreed,' said Ford, and the matter of payment for the job was discussed and settled.

'There's an empty building next to the livery stable,' said Ford. 'You can use that for your office. We'll move some furniture in and build a couple of cells inside.'

There was plenty of willing help available for the work, and with Jake supervising and also helping, it was finished four days later. To complete the operation identical signposts were erected beside the two trails leading into town. The notices read: ALL PERSONS ENTERING LARINO WITH FIREARMS MUST LEAVE THEM AT THE MARSHAL'S OFFICE WHILE IN TOWN. BY ORDER OF THE TOWN COUNCIL.

The Rocking P cook learnt of the ban when he drove a buckboard into town for supplies, and he took the news back to the ranch. The following morning three riders left the ranch and headed for Larino. They were Weaver, Verity and Trent. Weaver, a quick-tempered man, tall, slim and in his early thirties, was reckoned to be the best man with a six-gun at the ranch. His two companions, both shorter than he, were pretty handy with a six-gun themselves. But neither was in the same class as Weaver.

When the three riders reached the new signpost outside town, they halted, then Trent roped it with his lariat and brought it down. This action was observed by a homesteader called Varley, who was riding out of town at the time. He turned and rode quickly back to tell Jake what was happening.

Jake checked his Peacemaker, then walked out on to the street. He could see the three riders coming towards him. He stood in the middle of the street, facing them. Forty yards away, the three men dismounted and tied their horses to a hitching rail. Then Weaver walked along the middle of the street towards Jake, while his two partners moved to a position just outside the livery stable door, which was standing ajar. Apart from Jake and the three ranch hands, the street was completely deserted.

Jake saw that each of the three men was carrying a six-gun in a right-hand holster. He knew that he was in a dangerous situation. He felt confident of his ability to deal with Weaver, but to counter any intervention by the other two as well, without getting himself killed, was a difficult problem confronting him. He steeled himself for the task.

Weaver halted about nine yards from Jake and stood motionless, roughly abreast of his two partners. He was crouching slightly, his right hand close to his holster.

'I reckon you know about the new law,' said Jake. 'You can leave your gun in my office.'

'Like hell I will,' said Weaver. 'Nobody takes my gun away from me. But maybe you'd like to try?'

As he finished speaking he went for his gun and made the smoothest, speediest draw of which he was capable. But it was not good enough. He realized this as the bullet from Jake's Peacemaker struck him in the chest, near his right shoulder, before he was ready to trigger his own gun. He dropped his weapon and sank down with one knee on the ground.

Weaver's two partners saw that he had been hit. Before they could draw their guns they heard a shouted command behind them. Turning, they saw the liveryman standing in the doorway of the stable. He was holding a shotgun, with the hammer cocked, pointing directly at them. They knew the damage a shotgun blast at that range could do. They dropped their guns on the ground at Nelson's command.

Jake relaxed at the intervention which had possibly saved his life. He picked up the three guns and dropped them on the boardwalk near his office door. Then he walked over to Nelson, who

24

was still holding the shotgun on Verity and Trent.

'I owe you,' said Jake to the liveryman. 'I was in a bad situation there. Don't know how it would have ended if you hadn't taken a hand.'

He took Nelson aside, still keeping the ranch hands covered with his six-gun.

'I suppose you know,' he said, 'that there's no cartridge in the shotgun?'

'Sure I know,' said Nelson. 'I ain't got no cartridges. The shotgun had been left here when I took the stable over. I've never used it. But I didn't feel easy leaving you to face those three alone. I figured it was worth a try.'

'You're a brave man,' said Jake.

'To tell the truth,' said the liveryman, 'I was purty darned scared.'

'You weren't the only one,' said Jake. 'I'd be obliged if you'd watch the man I shot while I put the other two in one of the cells. He don't know your shotgun ain't loaded.'

When this had been done, Nelson gave Jake the names of the three prisoners. Then he told Jake, outside their hearing, that the homesteader, Varley, who had warned of the arrival of the three Rocking P hands, was the man who had reported seeing Bart Peary near the ranch.

'I thought maybe you'd like to speak with him,' said Nelson. 'I know him pretty well. I reckon you can trust him to keep his mouth shut.'

'I'd like a talk with him,' said Jake, 'but ask him if he'd mind waiting till I've had Weaver's wound tended to.'

He called Doc Trump, who had joined a group of onlookers on the street. 'Can you take a look at this man, Doc?' he asked.

'Business has sure been looking up since you hit town,' said Trump. 'Bring him along to my house.'

Two of the onlookers supported Weaver as he slowly followed Trump. Inside his house the doctor extracted a bullet, then treated and bandaged the wound.

'Nothing vital was hit,' said Trump, 'and it should heal up in time.'

'Can he ride back to the ranch?' asked Jake.

'Yes, if he takes it slow and easy,' the doctor replied.

Jake took the injured man to his office, and put him in the cell with his two companions.

'Each one of you,' he said, 'has got to pay a twenty-dollar fine for refusing to deposit your guns. Have you got the money on you?'

Seething with anger, the three men shook their heads.

'In that case,' said Jake, looking at Verity and Trent, 'one of you two had better ride to the ranch and bring me back sixty dollars. Then you can all three ride back to the ranch. And I want Jed Peary to know that I'm getting word to the US marshal in

Amarillo about what's happened here today. If there's any more trouble like that he'll be sending a deputy marshal to look into it.'

Trent departed a few minutes later, and Jake went to the livery stable to join the liveryman and Varley, the man who was running a homestead near the Rocking P. Varley told Jake that he had seen Bart Peary riding towards the ranch buildings a few days after Emma was killed, and that he had not seen him since.

'The reason I can recognize him at a distance,' he said, 'is because he has a certain way of sitting in the saddle. Slouches forward quite a bit.'

Jake thanked the homesteader for the information, and Varley, as he was leaving, said he would let him know if he sighted Bart Peary again.

'It looks like Bart might be at the ranch,' said Jake. 'I reckon I'll ride there after dark and see if I can find out. I can't bring the law in until I'm sure he's still there.'

'You need to be careful,' said the liveryman. 'If you get caught nosing around there alone, I reckon you'll be as good as dead.'

Later in the day Trent returned with the sixty dollars in payment of the fines.

'Mr Peary told me to let you know,' he said to Jake, 'that he's ordering all hands to leave their weapons with you as soon as they hit town.'

As Jake stood outside his office, watching the

27

three riders leave town, he was joined by the livery-man.

'I had a feeling that Peary would back down over this,' said Jake. 'I guess the last thing he wants is a deputy US marshal nosing around here.'

THREE

Jake left town an hour before dark, after advising Nelson that he was not sure when he would return. When the lights from inside the Rocking P ranch buildings showed through the darkness, he left his horse in a small hollow and approached the buildings on foot. The sky was overcast.

Cautiously, he slowly circled all the buildings and established that two guards had been posted outside the front door of the ranch house, and a third guard had been posted outside a small side door of the same building. As he stood motionless, considering his next move, he heard the cook calling the hands to supper.

He could see the cookshack door opening and closing as the hands went in, and he waited until they had finished their meal and had left the building. He waited a further fifteen minutes, then approached the unguarded side of the ranch house without being spotted by any of the three guards. He moved towards the front of the building, and lay flat on the ground, with his head close to the corner.

For a while there was no sound from the two guards nearby. Then one of them lit a cigarette and they started to chat. At first, Jake heard nothing of interest to himself. Then the conversation turned to a topic which grabbed his attention. The two men were talking about Bart Peary's recent arrival at the ranch, and speculating on the possibility of him joining up with his father for a while, as he had indicated he was thinking of doing. As the conversation continued for a while, Jake became certain that Jed Peary was running a criminal operation from the Rocking P.

When the conversation ceased, he decided to leave the ranch and enlist the help of the US marshal in Amarillo in arresting Bart Peary and closing down his father's operation. But before leaving, he decided to take a closer look at the other buildings, to gain information which might be useful on a future visit.

He retreated from the house, and went over to the cookshack, which was now in darkness. He walked round it. As he was passing along the side remote from the entrance door, his foot struck a low obstacle on the ground. He stepped over it, then, as he took another step forward, a rotted timber cover under his feet gave way and he dropped into a vertical well shaft, a little over two feet in diameter, which was no longer in use.

Unable to arrest his fall, he dropped down the shaft, his arms and legs bumping against the wall at various points, until his feet hit the bottom, which was soft and moist. He crouched there, assessing the damage caused by the fall. No bones were broken, but his right leg, which had hit the ground first, had been badly jarred, and was painful.

He stood up and listened. There was no indication that the sound of his fall had caught anyone's attention. He struck a match and looked around. He could see that the wall of the circular shaft was constructed of stones of various shapes and sizes, with thick layers of mortar between them. Running his hand up and down the surface, he could feel that it was fairly smooth. Through the top of the shaft, whose depth he estimated as at least eighteen feet, he could see the night sky. It was clear that his situation was desperate. Unless he could escape from the well before daylight came, his capture was almost inevitable. And escape was impossible without footholds on the wall of the shaft.

He took a stout hunting knife from his belt and drew the tip of the blade along the surface of one of the thick mortar joints. The mortar was not particularly hard, and he was able to dig the point of his knife-blade into it. As he did so, the mortar crumbled away. Relieved, he decided that escape was not impossible.

Using the point of his knife, and working by touch, he started digging footholds in the mortar joints at various points diametrically opposite one another on the wall of the shaft. It was vital that the footholds be secure, and progress was slow. He had little idea of the passage of time.

When he had fashioned as many footholds as was possible from a standing position at the bottom of the shaft, he paused to secure the knife to his wrist, using his bandanna for the purpose. Then, by means of the footholds he had already made, he slowly climbed up the shaft and dug out further footholds as he did so. Progress was much slower, and much more difficult than before.

He had risen about five feet above the bottom of the shaft when a piece of stone broke away beneath the edge of the sole of his right boot and once again he fell to the bottom of the shaft, aggravating the injury he had suffered earlier. He rested for a short while, then slowly climbed back up the shaft, locating the footholds, one by one, with his fingers. Progress was very slow, and by the time he regained the position that he had reached at the time of his last fall, the pain in his right leg was excruciating.

He continued making footholds, and climbing further up the shaft. Still some way from the top, he paused and looked upwards. With dismay, he saw that the sky above was growing lighter. Groaning with pain, he redoubled his efforts.

In the bunkhouse on the Rocking P the cook stirred in his bunk, and a few minutes later he rose and dressed. It was growing light outside, and he had much to do before calling the hands to breakfast an hour and a quarter later. Yawning, he left the bunkhouse and walked towards the cookshack. Just before passing one end of it, he glanced along the side, and noticed that the top of the disused well shaft appeared to be uncovered. Curious, he walked silently towards it, then halted before reaching it, as he heard a scraping sound coming from inside the shaft. A small man, in his sixties, who did not own a gun, he decided to get a couple of hands to investigate.

He went back to the bunkhouse and roused Trent and another hand called Armstrong. He told them about the noises in the old well shaft. They dressed quickly, buckled on their gun-belts, and followed the cook outside.

Inside the well, Jake finished making the last foothold which would bring him high enough to clamber out. He placed the sole of his boot on it, slowly raised his head above the top of the shaft, and looked around. Two six-guns were pointing directly at his head. He froze.

'Well I'm damned!' said Trent. 'If it ain't the new marshal of Larino. He's the one who shot Weaver in town yesterday, and fined the three of us. I reckon we should take him to Mr Peary right now.'

They took Jake's knife and six-gun, then Trent and Armstrong escorted him as he hobbled painfully to the ranch house, where Trent woke Jed Peary and told him about the intruder. The rancher dressed and went down to the spacious living room, where the prisoner was being held. He was a heavily built man, in his early sixties, bearded and hard-faced. He walked up to Jake and inspected him closely. Then he spoke to Armstrong.

'This man's horse must be around somewhere,' he said. 'Find it and bring it in.'

As he finished speaking, his son Bart joined them. Immediately, Jake recognized him as the man who had killed his wife.

'This man,' the rancher told his son, 'is the new marshal who fined us sixty dollars yesterday. And it seems that he trespassed on our property during the night, damaged a well cover, and fell down the shaft. All we know about him is that he drifted up here from Amarillo, and took on the job of marshal in Larino.'

He turned and spoke to Jake. His voice was hard.

'I'm glad you turned up here, Madison,' he said. 'You've saved me the job of picking you up in Larino before you caused me any more trouble. I don't want no town marshal in Larino, especially one that ain't in my pay. You were a fool to come out here on your own. Maybe you'd like to tell us just what you're doing here?'

Jake could think of no plausible explanation, other than the truth, of his presence in the well shaft just before dawn. He stayed silent. Looking at the man responsible for the death of his wife, he resisted an almost overpowering impulse to run over and take him by the throat.

'I figured not,' said the rancher, as he turned to Trent, who had been keeping the prisoner covered. He took Trent's six-gun.

'Go and bring another hand here,' he said, 'then take Madison to one of the stalls in the stable. Tie him up good and leave him there for now.'

When the two hands had departed with Jake, the rancher and his son discussed the situation.

'Madison has to die,' said Jed Peary, 'but not here. His death has got to look like an accident, and it's got to take place well away from the Rocking P. Latimer and Murray are riding south today to look the ground over in connection with a stagecoach robbery I'm planning later this month south of Amarillo. I'll get them to take Madison and get rid of him on the way.'

The pair discussed in detail the instructions to be given to the two men about the disposal of the prisoner.

'I'll tell them,' said Jed Peary, as the discussion ended, 'not to give Madison the idea they're going to kill him. They can take him a day's ride or so from here, then they can finish him off, like we just discussed.'

Lying on the floor, inside the stable, Jake was certain that Jed Peary's intention was to kill him because of the threat posed by Jake to his criminal activities. The only questions were, when and how? He was tightly trussed, and for the moment there was no chance of escape.

Three hours later he was unbound, except for the rope around his wrists, and was taken to the ranch house, where his horse was waiting. Standing close by were two other saddled horses, the Pearys, and Murray and Latimer.

'I don't want you anywhere near here, Madison,' said Jed Peary, 'so these two men are taking you for a long ride.'

He ordered Jake to mount, and Murray and Latimer did the same. The three horses moved off to the south, with Murray leading the prisoner's mount. The pain in Jake's right leg, which had been so intense as he was climbing up the well shaft, had eased considerably. They kept well away from the main trails leading south.

They camped out overnight, with Murray and Latimer guarding the prisoner in turn. On the following day, around noon, they stopped for a break, outside the house of what appeared to be an abandoned homestead. The building, stoutly built of timber, gave the appearance of having been deserted many years ago. The door was standing ajar. A creek bed, now completely dry, passed close by the house. Jake's guess was that the homestead had been abandoned because the water supply from the creek had dried up permanently some time in the past.

Latimer built a fire, and made some coffee. Jake was ordered to sit down. His hands were untied and he was handed some food and a mug of coffee. He felt certain that he was due to be killed sometime during the next few hours, and maybe his hands would not be freed again.

Exploding into action, he threw the contents of the mug into Murray's face, temporarily blinding him and scalding the flesh. Latimer went for his six-gun, but before he could bring it to bear on the prisoner, Jake had dodged round Murray's horse, which was standing between the three men and the house. He paused to pull Murray's rifle from the saddle holster, then ran towards the house, firing a shot towards Latimer as he did so. He saw Latimer's left hand go up to his ear, before he quickly recovered and sent a bullet from his six-gun, which slammed into the doorpost as Jake pushed the door open and entered the house, closing the door behind him.

Quickly, he examined the rifle. Relieved, he saw that there were still sixteen rounds in the magazine. He looked round the interior of the single-storey house. There were still a few items of furniture remaining, including a small table, solidly built, with one stout centre leg with splayed feet. There were two windows and a door at the front of the house, and one other window, in one side of the house.

Outside, the two men had separated. Latimer, his ear damaged by the passing bullet, had taken up position behind a small shed, still standing, from which he could see the front of the house and the side with the window. Murray, his face smarting badly, but with vision unimpaired, stood, cursing, against the other side of the house. Latimer aimed a few rifle bullets at the windows and the door, then decided to waste no more ammunition. He knew that if he and his partner tried to rush the house and shoot it out with Jake they were liable to end up dead. They would have to think up some other way of dealing with the situation.

As he was considering the matter, he saw Murray run from the blind side of the house to a nearby patch of brush. He cut out an armful with his knife and laid it at the foot of the side wall of the house. He cut five further bundles in succession, placing two more at the side of the house, and three at the foot of the rear wall. He signalled to Latimer, then, using matches, he lit all six bundles.

Both the brush and the house timbers were extremely dry, and the walls were soon burning fiercely, the flames spreading upwards. The two men outside watched closely for any attempt by Jake to escape from the burning building. Latimer was holding a rifle, Murray a six-gun.

Inside the house Jake was quickly aware of the new threat facing him. The inside of the building started filling with smoke, and he could see the flames rising up the side and rear walls. Still holding the rifle, he took up a temporary position under the table, with his head close to the floor, and his bandanna held over his nose and mouth. He knew that the two men outside were waiting to cut him down as soon as he attempted to leave the house.

The flames spread to the roof timbers, and Jake decided that he had no option but to leave the burning building and face the risks outside. He was just about to leave his position under the table when a burning roof beam fell on top of it. The table collapsed and Jake received a violent blow on the head. Just before losing consciousness he felt himself falling.

FOUR

Murray and Latimer kept a close watch on the burning building while the walls collapsed, the roof fell in, and the flames eventually started to subside.

'One thing's sure,' said Latimer. 'Madison ain't going to bother us no more.'

'That's right,' said Murray, 'but I sure wish he hadn't taken my rifle in there. That was a good rifle. Must be ruined by now. No point in wasting any more time here. We might as well carry on south.'

Latimer agreed and they walked over to the horses which were standing close to the shed that Latimer had been using for cover earlier. They stood there for a while, discussing the job they had been ordered to do after their prisoner had been disposed of.

Their backs were to the door of the shed, and they did not see it opening. But they heard the creak, and swung round, startled, to stare unbelievingly at the unwavering barrel of a rifle in the hands of the man who, they could have sworn, was lying dead in the smoking remains of the house nearby. They both froze.

'It don't make much difference to me,' said Jake, 'whether I hand you over to the law, or shoot you both dead right now. So from now on, you'd better do exactly like I tell you. Raise your hands as high as they'll go and stand with your faces against the side of the shed there.'

The two men complied and Jake took their six-guns. He kept one of them, after checking it, then threw the other one, and the rifle, aside. Silently, he walked up behind the two men, and quickly delivered a carefully judged blow to each of their heads with the barrel of his six-gun. The blows were designed to stun the recipients for a short while.

Murray and Latimer both collapsed on the ground, and Jake tied their hands behind them, using a length of rope he had seen in the shed. He sat down to await their recovery, reflecting on an interesting piece of information received while he was inside the shed listening to the conversation between the two men. He had suspected that they were somewhere to the east of Amarillo, and this had been confirmed. Also, he had learnt that Amarillo was only about ten miles distant. He rose and collected the two lariats which were hanging from the saddles of the mounts belonging to his two prisoners.

The two men came round within a few minutes of one another. After a short while Jake turned them over and pulled them to their feet. Using the two lariats, he placed and tightened up a noose around each of their necks, then fastened the ends of the ropes to the horn of his saddle. He mounted his horse, and leading the other two mounts, he ordered the prisoners to start walking ahead of him in the direction of Amarillo, after reminding them of the extreme itchiness of his trigger finger. Cursing, they started trudging westward.

It was late afternoon when they reached the outskirts of Amarillo. Jake paused to speak to an old-timer standing outside a shack by the trail. He asked him where the US marshal's office was located. The old man looked curiously at the two prisoners.

'Carry straight on,' he said, 'and you'll see it on the left, just past the livery stable.'

Jake thanked him and proceeded along the street, attracting a small group of onlookers as he did so.

Seated at a desk inside his office, US Marshal Ryan glanced out of the window. He saw two men standing on the street, with hands tied, and ropes around their necks. He rose quickly and walked outside. Jake dismounted and went up to him.

'Howdy, Marshal,' he said. 'My name's Madison. These—'

Ryan interrupted him. 'Madison?' he said. 'Would you happen to be the ex-town marshal of Wildern in Wyoming?'

Jake nodded.

'Only this morning,' said Ryan, 'one of my deputies rode in from Denver. He heard from Tom Nelson, who used to be sheriff there, that you figured you might catch up with Bart Peary in the Panhandle.'

'That's right,' said Jake, 'and I found him on his father's ranch.'

'Just a minute,' said the marshal. 'You've got charges against these two men?'

Jake confirmed this, and Ryan called on a deputy to put Murray and Latimer into a jail cell. Then he and Jake went into the office and sat down at the desk. Ryan, a tall, rangy man in his fifties, and wearing a neat goatee beard, expressed his sympathy with Jake over the tragic loss of his wife. Then he listened with considerable interest to Jake's account of events since his recent arrival in Larino.

'That's mighty interesting,' said the marshal, when Jake had finished, 'but you ain't explained just how you managed to get out of that burning building alive.'

'It was pure luck,' said Jake. 'I figure that the homesteader who used to live there had a wife and maybe a child or two. And he was scared there might be an Indian raid, and the house might be burnt down with him and his family inside. So he built a tunnel, shored up with timber, from the inside of the house to the floor of a shed that was standing nearby.

'Inside the house there was a trapdoor in the floor, over the tunnel, with a table standing on it. I was sheltering under the table, and when a roof beam fell on it and broke the trapdoor, I fell down into the tunnel, and crawled along it to the shed.'

'I'm bringing the Texas Rangers in on this,' said Ryan. 'I'll have a word with Captain Jardine. This is our chance to get our hands on Bart Peary and his father. We won't give out any information about you and the two men you brought here, in case the news gets back to the Pearys before the rangers get there. Their visit to the Rocking P has got to be unexpected.'

'I'd like to go along,' said Jake.

'I reckon they'll be glad to have you,' said Ryan. 'I'll suggest that they swear you in as a ranger for the operation.'

'From what I overheard the two prisoners saying,' said Jake, 'I'm pretty sure that Jed Peary is running a sizeable criminal operation. I think he's sheltering a number of criminals on the Rocking P, all of them probably wanted men. And I reckon he's sending them out on various criminal operations planned by himself.'

'If you're right,' said the marshal, 'this operation could put some major criminals out of business. Let's go and see Jardine.'

They found the ranger captain in his office, and Ryan introduced Jake, then explained the situation. Jardine listened with interest.

'We'd be mighty glad to get hold of Bart Peary alone,' he said. 'We've been after him for a long time. And I sure like the prospect of capturing a few more criminals at the same time. I'm going to get as many rangers together as I can, and they'll leave early tomorrow and raid the Rocking P during the night.'

He turned to Jake. 'We'll be glad of your help,' he said, 'especially since you've been to the ranch recently.'

He proceeded to swear Jake in, and told him that the man in charge of the operation would be an experienced ranger called Hunter. He suggested that Jake took a room at the hotel nearby, and had a meal and some rest before leaving with the posse. Glad to follow this suggestion, Jake took his horse to the livery stable, then walked along to the hotel. After taking a meal, he went up to his room for some sleep.

A ranger roused him at daybreak, and after a

hurried breakfast he joined the rangers outside Jardine's office, collecting his horse on the way. The posse numbered eight, including himself. Hunter spoke with him about the exact location of the Rocking P, and the positioning of guards that Jake had seen during his recent visit. Following this, they discussed the way the operation was to be carried out. Then the posse left town.

They timed their arrival at the Rocking P for one o'clock in the morning. The night was dark. The posse stopped just before the two guards at the front of the house were visible.

'Hello the house,' shouted Hunter. 'I'm leading a posse of Texas Rangers. I want to speak to Jed Peary. Two of us are going to ride in closer.'

He repeated the call twice, and the answer came back to approach, but not too close. Hunter and another ranger called Martin dismounted and advanced until they could see the two guards. One of them was facing the wall by the side of the door, and he turned round as the two rangers came to a halt. The other guard called out for them to stay where they were while he went for the rancher.

Five minutes later he returned with Jed Peary, who asked Hunter what he wanted.

'There are more rangers behind me,' said Hunter. 'We have information that your son Bart Peary might be on the Rocking P. He's wanted for a number of robberies and killings. His latest job

47

was in Wildern, Wyoming, where he robbed the bank and killed an innocent woman bystander. We aim to find out whether he's here.'

'I'm afraid,' said Peary, 'that Bart and I parted a while ago. I never figured, when he left home, that he'd turn into a robber and a killer. I made it absolutely clear to him that he ain't welcome here.'

'All the same,' said Hunter, 'we'd like to take a look round.'

'Sure,' said Peary, as he was joined by his foreman, Lindsay, who had been absent from the ranch at the time of Jake's recent visit. 'You've got your job to do. Call your men up, and my foreman here will take you anywhere you want to go. I'll see you in the living room in the house, when you've finished.'

Hunter called to the other rangers to come up, and they all joined him except Jake, who remained where he was, out of sight of the ranch buildings, Hunter and the others carried out a thorough search of all the ranch buildings, including the barn and stable. When this had been completed, Hunter asked the foreman to tell Jed Peary that he would be coming into the house shortly to see him. Then the ranger walked to the place where Jake was waiting.

'There ain't no sign of Bart Peary,' he said, 'and as far as I can tell, there ain't any of those wanted criminals that you figured might be hiding out here. The bunkhouse is about the right size to sleep the number of men needed to run a cattle ranch like this. There are three bedrooms in the house, one not in use. Peary and his foreman are in the other two.

'So it looks like we ain't going to be able to capture the number of criminals we were hoping to. We'll arrest Peary for ordering your murder and harbouring his son. And we'll take his foreman in as well. He must have known what Jed Peary was doing. Let's go and see them now.'

Hunter went into the house with Jake and Martin, leaving the other rangers outside. Jed Peary and his foreman were seated alone in the living room awaiting the arrival of Hunter. It would be a big understatement to say that when the rangers walked in, Peary was surprised to see Jake. His eyebrows shot up, his jaw dropped, and he looked as though he had seen a ghost. He started to rise to his feet, then sank back in his chair as he saw the guns in the rangers' hands. Hunter spoke to him.

'You're in real trouble, Peary,' he said. 'We're taking you and your foreman prisoner. You'll be riding back to Amarillo with us. We already have the two men you ordered to kill Mr Madison.'

Peary opened his mouth to speak, then changed his mind. He glared at the rangers. Martin walked up and secured the hands of the two prisoners. Hunter called in another ranger to help Martin guard the two men, then he and Jake, with the remaining rangers, went to the bunkhouse, where all the hands were assembled. Hunter told them that Jed Peary and his foreman had been arrested and would be taken to Amarillo. As for them, he said that they were under suspicion of helping Peary in his criminal activities. He told them not to leave the ranch so long as investigations were under way.

Hunter and Jake returned to the house. It was just after sunrise. As they approached the door Jake noticed a box fixed to the wall against the doorpost. Curious, he stopped, pulled open a small door on the front of the box, and he and Hunter looked inside it. A telegraph key, of the type used in telegraph offices throughout the country, was standing on the bottom of the box. Puzzled, Jake looked around. He could see no telegraph poles supporting a wire to which the key could be connected.

'This ain't here for sending messages from the ranch to some place outside,' he said. 'But what *is* it for?'

'I've just remembered,' said Hunter, 'that when I first walked up to speak to Peary, I saw a guard standing here, facing this box. Maybe he was operating the key.'

'If that's so,' said Jake, 'I wonder where the signals were going? Let's find out.'

As he looked inside the box he could see two wires attached to the key. They disappeared through a hole in the back of the box, and he found them coming through the wall inside the house. They were fastened to the wall at intervals, and he and Hunter traced them until they passed through the wall of a storeroom. He entered the room and lit an oil lamp which he found inside. With its help, he traced the wires until they passed through a hole in the timber floor.

He pulled aside a piece of carpet covering the floor at this point, revealing a trapdoor. On it was a recessed ring which could be used for lifting the door upwards. Jake reached for the ring, and pulled the edge of the door open a few inches. By the light of the lamp, he and Hunter could see some steps leading downwards.

'Let's see what's down there,' said Hunter.

Jake closed the trapdoor, then turned to his companion.

'Maybe that ain't such a good idea,' he said. 'Maybe those wanted men I figured might be on the ranch, are down there. Maybe the telegraph key was put there so that the guard could give them a quick warning if there was a sudden raid by the law during the night. Then they would know that they needed to stay there in hiding. If I'm right, they could be waiting down there, ready to shoot down any stranger who went down those steps.'

'You're right,' said Hunter. 'We've got to think of some way of getting them out without any gunplay.'

'The way those steps are leading,' said Jake, 'it looks like they've built some accommodation under the ground outside the house. Let's go out there and see if there's any sign of it.'

They left the house and looked at the ground outside the wall of the storeroom. They found the ends of eight vertical metal pipes, not previously noticed in the dark, projecting just above ground level. Each pipe was covered by a removable cowl.

'I'm sure these are for ventilation,' said Jake. 'There are people down there. I hope Bart Peary's one of them. And I have an idea how we can get them out without anybody getting killed.'

He explained his plan to Hunter, who agreed to adopt it. The foreman was taken to the bunkhouse, and three rangers were assigned to guard him and the hands, whose weapons had been taken. One ranger accompanied Jake and Hunter to the house, where Jed Peary was still being held. They all went into the living room. Hunter walked up to Peary.

'We've found the steps leading down from the storeroom, Peary,' he said, 'and we're pretty sure that some of your friends are hiding down there. We're aiming to get them out without any blood being spilt. That's where you come in. You're going down those steps in front of us, and you're going to tell the men down there to leave their weapons behind and come out, one by one.'

'You're crazy,' said Peary. 'It won't work. I know the men down there. You'll have to go in after them.'

'We don't think so,' said Jake. 'We noticed some sticks of dynamite in a box in that shed near the barn. You'll tell the men down there that if they don't come out, one by one, unarmed, we're going to start dropping sticks of dynamite down the ventilator pipes. They'll have five minutes to make up their minds after they've been told. And that's something you're going to do right now.'

Peary was taken into the storeroom, where the trapdoor was pulled open. Jake and Hunter held Peary tightly from behind and forced him down the steps. At the bottom there was a dark passage leading away from the house. Peary halted, and called out along the passage.

'You there, Verity?' he shouted. Twice he repeated the call before the answer came.

'This is Verity. Is that you, Mr Peary?'

'Yes,' shouted Peary. 'I want to speak with Gorman, right now.'

Hunter and Jake exchanged glances. There was

a criminal gang, led by a man called Gorman, which had operated extensively in Texas and New Mexico Territory.

A few minutes later they heard Gorman's voice.

'What in hell's going on up there, Peary?' he shouted.

Jed Peary, inwardly seething with anger over the humiliating position in which he now found himself, tersely explained the situation to Gorman, telling him that unless he and the others started coming out, singly and unarmed, with hands raised, during the next five minutes, sticks of dynamite, with the fuse-cords ignited, would be dropped down the ventilation pipes.

He paused while Hunter gave him a further order to pass on. Then he also told Gorman that if there was any resistance as they came out, they would be shot down.

Hunter then spoke to Gorman. 'This is Ranger Hunter,' he called out. 'This is no bluff. You have five minutes, starting now.'

Four minutes later, as Peary stood at the bottom of the steps, with Jake and Hunter behind him, each of them holding a six-gun, Gorman himself appeared, walking along the passage with hands raised. Hunter recognized him immediately. The outlaw's hands were secured, and he was placed, under guard, in the living room.

One by one a further eight followed. All were

secured and taken into the living room. From 'wanted' posters that Hunter had studied, he was fairly confident that they included the other two members of the Gorman gang, as well as the three members of the equally notorious Slater gang.

'We'd better make sure there's nobody left down there,' said Jake, disappointed that Bart Peary was not among the captured men. He and Hunter, pushing Jed Peary in front of them, walked along the passage to the underground accommodation, lit by oil lamps. It consisted of fourteen well-furnished bedrooms, a living room, dining room and kitchen. They were all empty. In one of the bedrooms they found a battery and tele-graph sounder, to which the two wires from the telegraph key near the door of the house were connected. They took Jed Peary back into the house, to join the other prisoners there. Then Hunter took Jake aside.

'I guess you're disappointed that Bart Peary ain't among the men we've caught,' he said, 'but all the same, we've had a real good result from this operation. I'm sure we have the Gorman and Slater gangs among the ones we've just captured. As for the rest, I don't recognize them.'

'The one called Verity works for Jed Peary,' said Jake, 'and that probably applies to the other two as well. I know that Jed Peary had his own men work-ing on criminal operations. Maybe he was doing some of the planning for the Slater and Gorman gangs, as well as sheltering them.'

Hunter dispatched a ranger to Larino to send a telegraph message to Amarillo, requesting that a jail wagon be sent to pick up Jed Peary and his foreman, together with the Gorman and Slater gangs. The other men found at the ranch were to be guarded, pending a decision on whether they be charged.

Jake helped to guard the jail wagon on its journey back to Amarillo, and he later joined the ranger captain as he questioned each of the prisoners individually. But during the questioning all the prisoners denied any knowledge of the present whereabouts of Bart Peary.

Jake, still determined to hunt down the killer of his wife, had no idea where to start looking. Although the date of the trial had not yet been fixed, he decided to stay in Amarillo till the prisoners had been sentenced. Six days later, two days before the trial was due to be held, Captain Jardine called him into his office.

'Figured you'd like to know,' he said, 'that we just got news that Bart Peary was definitely identified as the man who robbed the Wells Fargo office in Pueblo, Colorado, two days ago. He took some gold that was awaiting shipment, and near killed the agent. A posse took off after him, but he got clean away. The agent reckons he might have shot

Peary in the arm.'

'I'm leaving for Pueblo right now,' said Jake. 'Maybe I can pick up Peary's trail. It looks like he changed his mind, and decided not to join up with his father.'

When Jake reached Pueblo, he went to the sheriff's office and introduced himself to Sheriff Grant, a respected lawman, nearing sixty.

'I heard about you helping to capture the Slater and Gorman gangs, as well as Jed Peary,' said Grant. 'And I know you're after Bart Peary, and why. All I can tell you is that it was definitely him, that he was probably wounded in the arm, and that when he left town he was heading south-east before he vanished without trace.'

Jake thanked the sheriff and left. He had decided that he would leave Pueblo the following morning, and would head south-east, in an effort to find some trace of his quarry.

FIVE

On the same day that Bart Peary had robbed the Wells Fargo office in Pueblo, widow Martha Denny was working on the small vegetable patch outside the house on her homestead south-east of Pueblo. Her nine-year-old son Billy was working on a small chore in one of the fields on the quarter section. Her husband had died of cholera three months earlier, and she had almost decided to move back with Billy to Illinois, where she had been born. She had more than enough money in the house to enable her to do this.

As she straightened up and looked towards Billy she saw, beyond him, a rider moving fast towards the homestead.

Bart Peary, who could see Martha working near the house, stopped as he came close to Billy. The boy noticed that the shirtsleeve on the man's left arm was torn and bloodstained.

'Howdy, boy,' said Peary. 'I just had an accident.

Could do with some help. Is your pa around?'

'No,' replied Billy. 'Pa's dead. Me and my ma are running the homestead. Maybe she can help you. Tell her I'll soon be finished here.'

Peary rode on, and stopped close to Martha Denny. He dismounted from the big chestnut he was riding. She saw the blood on his shirtsleeve.

'The boy told me there was no man around,' said Peary, 'so I'm going to tell you just what you have to do if you don't want you and him to get hurt. I've just had a run-in with the law, and I reckon there's a posse not far behind me. I've got a flesh wound on my arm that's been bleeding pretty bad. I want you to tend to that wound right now, then I aim to stay here in hiding for a few days, till it's safe for me to move on. You give me any trouble, and the boy's the one who'll suffer first. You understand?'

Martha nodded, and a moment later Billy ran up to see what was happening.

'This stranger has hurt his arm, Billy,' said Martha. 'I'm going to tend to it, and he'll be staying with us for a few days.'

Peary took his rifle from the saddle holster, then pointed to a small grove of trees, about a mile to the west.

'What I want you to do right now, Billy,' he said, 'is water my horse, then ride it to the middle of those trees over there. Take the saddle and bridle off, and tether it good. Take some fodder with you, and leave it there for the horse. Then you can walk back here.'

Surprised at the request, Billy looked at his mother. She nodded. 'As quick as you can, Billy,' she said.

Peary and the woman went into the house, and the outlaw found an unloaded six-gun and rifle, of which he took charge. Then he sat on a chair near a window through which he had a clear view to the north-west. Martha cleaned the wound, put a pad over it, and held this in place with a length of bandage. Peary then told her to prepare some food for him. He was eating this, still sitting by the window, when Billy returned. Billy's mother told him to stay inside.

It was an hour and a half later when Peary caught sight of six or seven riders in the distance, heading in their direction. Billy's mother told him to go in one of the bedrooms with Peary, and not to make any noise if the approaching riders called at the homestead. Peary and Billy went into the bedroom, the outlaw taking with him the weapons and his bloodstained shirt and vest, which had both been replaced by ones previously belonging to Billy's dead father. He threw the shirt and vest in to the bottom of a cupboard standing against the wall. Then they both waited in silence, Billy wondering who the man was, and why his mother was behaving so strangely.

Sheriff Grant led his posse straight to the Denny homestead. As the riders stopped outside the house, Martha Denny came out.

'We're chasing an outlaw called Peary, Mrs Denny,' said the sheriff. 'Happen he called here earlier today, or you saw him riding by? He was riding a big chestnut, with a white stripe down its face.'

'Ain't seen nobody all day,' she said. 'What did this Peary do?'

'Robbed the Wells Fargo office in Pueblo,' Grant replied, 'and badly wounded the agent. We'd best be moving on.'

He looked around. 'Where's young Billy?' he asked.

'He's laid up with a fever,' she replied. 'If it don't get any better soon, I'm going into Pueblo for the doctor.'

Grant dismounted, and walked up to her.

'I hope that ain't going to be necessary,' he said. 'I'll go in and have a few words with him.'

'He'd like that,' said Martha Denny, 'but he's asleep just now, and maybe you shouldn't risk picking up whatever it is that Billy's got.'

Grant hesitated, then turned and climbed back on his horse. 'You're right,' he said. 'We'll be on our way.'

The posse rode on towards the south-east, and

soon after they had left, Peary put his rifle, and the weapons he had found in the house, on top of the cupboard in the bedroom, out of reach of the boy and his mother. He was carrying a six-gun in a right-hand holster. Then he and Billy went to join Martha Denny.

Peary told her that he aimed to stay four nights at the homestead. He and Billy would sleep in the bedroom they had just left, with the door fastened on the inside. She could use the smaller bedroom. During the day, either she, or her boy, or both, had to be close to him at any particular time.

Billy was beginning to understand what was happening. The stranger was being chased by the group of riders which had just called at the homestead. And he was intending to stay in hiding at the homestead for a few more nights, against the wishes of Billy's mother. Staring at Peary, he walked over to her, and she put an arm around his shoulder.

'It's all right, Billy,' she said. 'We'll do what this man says, and nobody'll get hurt. You can sleep on a mattress on the floor.'

'You do like your ma told you, Billy,' said Peary, 'and everything's going to be fine. One thing I want you to do tomorrow is bring my horse back here, and fasten it in the barn, out of sight.'

By the morning of Peary's intended departure there had been no callers at the homestead since the posse left. Martha Denny had been tending to the outlaw's wound, which was healing well. Just prior to his departure he was in the kitchen with Billy and his mother. He had found no cash in the house during his previous search for weapons. And he had his eye on a tin box standing on a shelf near the stove. Suspecting that this box contained cash, he took it down and opened it, then took out the fat roll of banknotes which it contained.

'No!' shouted Martha Denny. 'We need that money to get back East.'

Peary ignored her, and frantically, as he replaced the empty box on the shelf, she rushed at him, in an effort to regain the notes. He slapped her hard on the side of the face. As she fell sideways her head slammed against the solid metal top of the stove and she collapsed, unconscious.

Billy ran up to help his mother, but Peary struck him hard on the side of his jaw, and the boy, stunned, fell to the floor. When he recovered he found himself tied hand and foot. His mother lay motionless on the floor, with an angry bruise on the side of her head.

There was no sign of Peary. He had already left the homestead, leading off the two horses kept there. Before heading off to the south-east he collected the proceeds of the robbery from a patch of brush in which he had hidden them on his way to the homestead.

It took Billy just over an hour to free himself. His mother had remained motionless, and had not responded to his efforts to talk with her. He knelt down by her side. Her eyes were closed and she did not seem to be breathing. He must get help. He decided to ride to the nearest homestead, six miles to the north-west. He tried once again, unsuccessfully, to rouse his mother, then went out for a horse. Finding them both missing, and close to panic, he started off, on foot, to seek help.

In Pueblo Jake had learnt from Sheriff Grant that the posse chasing Bart Peary had stopped well short of the border with Indian Territory when they had failed to find anybody who had seen the outlaw. Jake decided to carry the search into the Indian Territory if necessary.

Leaving Pueblo, he headed south-east. At a point where the Denny homestead was two miles ahead of him, he saw a small figure, alternately running and walking, approaching him. He quickened his pace, and when he reached Billy, he stopped and dismounted. He could see the worry and despair on the face of the boy standing in front of him.

'You in trouble, boy?' he asked.

'It's my ma,' said Billy, 'back there in the house. She's lying on the floor. She ain't moving, and she ain't talking to me. Can you help her, mister?'

'Tell me what happened later,' said Jake, lifting the boy on to the horse behind the saddle. 'Hold on tight.'

He climbed into the saddle, and rode on fast to the homestead. He ran into the kitchen with Billy and knelt beside the woman lying on the floor. Almost immediately, he established that she was dead. He turned to Billy.

'Your mother has died,' he said. 'As soon as you feel like it, you can tell me what happened here.'

The tears welled up in Billy's eyes, and he started sobbing. Jake put an arm around his shoulders until the crying stopped. Then, haltingly, Billy gave an account of events which had taken place since the outlaw's arrival at the homestead. His story left no doubt in Jake's mind that the man who had hidden at the homestead was Bart Peary.

'What we'll do, Billy,' said Jake, 'is ride to Pueblo to see the sheriff and to get somebody to come here for your mother and take her back there. But first, I'll have a look around here.'

He went into the bedroom which Peary had used. Upon opening the cupboard he saw the bloodstained vest and shirt lying at the bottom. He picked up the vest and patted the pockets. They seemed to be empty, but feeling inside with his fingers, he found a small slip of paper in one of them. He pulled it out, and took it over to the window to examine it. Scrawled on it faintly, in pencil, was 'DONOVAN. BRODY. 14TH'. He continued his search, but found nothing else of interest.

On reaching Pueblo they went straight to the sheriff's office. Grant looked surprised as he saw them enter. He was even more surprised, and shocked, when Jake told him about Peary's stay on the Denny homestead, and the death of Billy's mother.

'Damn!' said the sheriff. 'His horse wasn't around, so we never figured he'd be inside the house. I'll get somebody to go for the body right now.'

Jake took Billy outside, then asked him to wait there a few minutes while he went back to see the sheriff. Inside the office again, he spoke to Grant.

'I'm worried about the boy,' he said. 'Has he got any kin you know of?'

'I happen to know that he hasn't,' Grant replied, 'neither out here or back East.'

'In that case,' said Jake, 'I'd like to take care of him, after I've hunted Bart Peary down. Meantime, is there any family in Pueblo he could stay with while I finish the job?'

'I reckon widow Ramsey would be happy to have him,' said Grant. 'She was a friend of Martha Denny. Runs a laundry just along the street. Has a big heart, and a boy and a girl, both around the same age as Billy. Leave Billy in here with me for a spell, and go and see her.'

Jake went outside, and told Billy that the same man who had killed Billy's mother had also killed his own wife, and that he was aiming to capture him and hand him over to the law.

'When I've done that, Billy,' he said, 'I'd like to look after you, if that's what you want. Meantime, I was figuring to ask Mrs Ramsey if you could stay with her till I get back. Is that all right with you?'

Near to tears, Billy looked up at Jake. 'I guess so,' he said. 'Will you be back soon?'

'Just as soon as I can, Billy,' Jake replied. 'Now you stay with the sheriff for a spell, while I see Mrs Ramsey.'

He found her in the laundry, a plump, motherly, cheerful woman.

Shocked, she listened while Jake told her of the events at the homestead. Then he told her of the death of his wife and unborn child, followed by his pursuit of the outlaw.

'I heard that Billy has no kin alive,' he said, 'and if he's agreeable, I'd like to adopt him as soon as I've dealt with Peary. Meanwhile, I'm here to ask if you'd look after him till I get back? I'll be paying for his room and board, and anything else he needs.'

'Of course I'll look after him,' said Mrs Ramsey. 'Poor boy, to lose both parents in a short time like that. Is he in town?'

'He's with the sheriff,' said Jake. 'I'm going there now. I'll send Billy to you right away.'

When Billy left for the laundry, Jake stayed behind, and showed the sheriff the slip of paper he had taken from the pocket in Bart Peary's vest. Grant studied it closely.

'It could be to do,' said Jake, 'with a meeting between Peary and somebody. DONOVAN is probably a man's name, and maybe BRODY is a place, though I can't say I've heard of it. And maybe the 14TH means the fourteenth of this month, which is three days from now.'

'I don't recall ever hearing of a place called Brody,' said the sheriff, 'but let's go and ask the telegraph operator.'

At the telegraph office, the operator found 'Brody' on a list of place names, on which it was shown as being in the Indian Territory. He produced a tattered map, and showed them the location of Brody, in the north-west of the territory. They thanked the operator, and went back to the sheriff's office.

'I know I'm doing a lot of guessing here,' said Jake, 'but Peary *was* heading in the direction of Brody. I'm going to ride there. Maybe I'll get lucky.'

The sheriff wished him well.

Jake went to the funeral of Martha Denny the

following day. She was buried in the cemetery on the edge of town. Townspeople and homesteaders attended. After the ceremony, Jake had a few words with Billy. He told him that he was leaving to search for the outlaw, but would come back for him just as soon as he could.

SIX

On the fourteenth day of the month, the day on which Jake was aiming to arrive in Brody, Ellen Newman, wife of Brody storekeeper Mark Newman was out riding, north-west of town. Born thirty years earlier, in Montana, and a keen horsewoman, one of her favourite pastimes was a ride out on her handsome bay gelding, a gift from her husband. Now heading back towards Brody, she was approaching a flat-topped hill, unaware that she was under scrutiny.

An outlaw on the run called Miller was observing her approach with considerable interest. Four miles to the north, his horse had suffered a broken leg, and he had walked to the hill, where he decided to take a rest in a gully running down the side. It was imperative that he should get hold of another mount as quickly as possible.

He was totally unaware that both he and the

approaching rider were being watched by Jake, who had ridden his horse to the top of the hill earlier. He was resting in a hollow there, intending to ride into Brody after dark.

Miller ran out of the gully in front of the woman rider cantering towards him. He fired a shot in the air from the six-gun he was holding in his hand. The startled horse reared, and it was a little while before the rider could bring it under control. Then Miller ran up and grabbed the reins, pointing his six-gun at the woman.

'Get off the horse,' he said, 'or I'll shoot you out of the saddle. I need this animal for myself, and I ain't particular what I have to do to get it.'

Ellen Newman, a slim attractive woman, looked down at the outlaw. He was a stocky man, dirty and unkempt, with a swarthy repellent face. She felt no doubt that he would carry out his threat. She dismounted, wondering whether he would shoot her just the same.

But it seemed that his intentions were otherwise. He dropped the reins, slapped Ellen hard on the face with his left hand, and threw her to the ground. As he knelt down beside her, trying to pin her down, Jake was running up behind him, with the intention of pistol-whipping him on the head. But he was still a dozen paces away when he stumbled as one foot came down on a loose piece of rock lying on the ground.

71

Miller grabbed his gun and swung round as he heard the noise, and the two men fired simultaneously. As a bullet passed harmlessly by Jake's left ear, Miller staggered back under the impact of a bullet which lodged in his heart. Then he collapsed. Jake ran up and took his weapon. Briefly, he knelt down by the outlaw. Then he went over to the woman, who was sitting up. Badly shaken, she was staring at the motionless body on the ground.

'You all right?' he asked.

'I am, thanks to you,' she replied. 'Lucky for me you happened along. Is he dead?'

'He is,' said Jake. 'I was aiming to pistol-whip him, but he heard me coming and I had to shoot him.'

He helped her to her feet. She told him that she was on the way back to Brody, about three miles distant, where she and her husband ran the general store. Jake told her that he would stay at the scene until she arranged for somebody in town to pick up the body.

'As soon as I get back,' she said, 'I'll tell the undertaker to come out here with a buckboard as soon as he can.'

Jake could see that the woman was recovering from the shock of her recent ordeal. He decided to take her into his confidence. He told her the reasons for his presence there, and described Bart

Peary. He asked her if she had seen Peary in Brody recently, and whether she knew a man called Donovan.

She shook her head. 'I'm sorry,' she said. 'In both cases the answer is "No". You'll be riding into town with the undertaker?'

'Yes,' Jake replied. 'It'll be dark by then. Less chance of Peary seeing me if he's in town. I'd be obliged if you don't mention to anybody, except your husband, the reason why I'm here.'

'All right,' she said. 'When you reach town come and see us at the store. You can have a meal with us, and maybe my husband can help you find the two men you're looking for.'

She rode off shortly after, and Jake stayed there until the undertaker arrived just before dark. When the body had been loaded on to the buckboard Jake rode on ahead, into town. He rode along the single deserted street and stopped when he reached the store. There was a CLOSED notice in the window. Leaving his horse at the hitching rail, he walked round to the door of the living quarters at the rear of the store. His knock was answered by Ellen Newman, who invited him in and introduced her husband.

'We've sure got a lot to thank you for,' said Newman, an energetic, pleasant-looking man, around the same age as his wife. 'From now on, any rides out of town will be taken by the two of us together. You reckon the man you shot was an outlaw?'

'Almost certainly,' Jake replied. 'He must have lost his horse somehow. It's clear he was desperate to get hold of another one, even if he had to kill to get it. The undertaker is on his way back here with the body. Should be arriving soon.'

A little later they had supper, and when it was over Jake gave them a full account of all the events leading up to his presence in Brody.

'I'm sure,' said Newman, 'that there's nobody called Donovan living in town or in the area around here. As for the man Peary you told us about, I'm going out now to check with the folks in town whether anybody's seen him today or earlier. I'll make up some story about the reason I want to know. Stay here. I'll be back soon.'

Newman returned half an hour later.

'Peary,' he said, 'hasn't been seen in the livery stable, saloon, hotel, or blacksmith shop. So it don't look like he's in town. And like me, none of the folks I spoke to has heard of a man called Donovan around here. So it looks like you guessed wrong about Peary turning up in Brody.'

'I'm beginning to think you're right,' said Jake, 'but I'll take a room at the hotel for a few days, just in case he turns up.'

'If Peary is spotted by any of the folk I spoke to in town,' said Newman, 'I'll be told. I'll pass the information on to you. As for the man who attacked Ellen, we'll bury him in the cemetery, and report the matter to the first US deputy marshal who calls in here.'

During the morning of the following day two men were talking in a shack on the outskirts of Brody. Behind it, in a small tall-fenced enclosure, were two horses. One of the men inside was known to the townspeople as Fox, although his real name was Donovan. He was wanted for robbery and murder in Arizona Territory. Seeking refuge in the Indian Territory, he had arrived in Brody two months earlier, and had rented the shack. His story was that he was a drifter by nature, but had decided to settle down for a spell, until he got the urge to move on again. He appeared to be well provided for, financially.

The man with him was Bart Peary, an old friend of his. Peary knew about Donovan taking the shack, and also its exact location. He had arrived there during the night, with the intention of discussing the possibility of a partnership in crime.

'I've got some news for you,' said Donovan. 'I've just been talking with the barkeep at the saloon. It seems he overheard the storekeeper asking the owner of the saloon whether he'd seen a man in town. The man he described was you, down to the scar, and the name he gave was yours. Then he asked the owner if he knew of a man called Donovan anywhere in the area. He got a negative answer to each question.'

'Damnation!' shouted Peary. 'How in hell did the storekeeper come to think that both of us might be here?'

'I don't know,' said Donovan, a big, bearded man, whose jovial appearance belied his true nature. 'And there was something else happened yesterday. I don't see how, but maybe the two things are connected. The storekeeper's wife was out riding, when a man on foot tried to take her horse. A stranger called Madison, who was heading for Brody, saw what was happening, and killed the horse thief before he could get away. I saw Madison this morning, taking his horse to the blacksmith.'

'Tell me what he looks like,' said Peary, fearing the worst.

When Donovan had done this, Peary told him that the man he had just described was the one responsible for the arrest of Peary's father and the Slater and Gorman gangs.

'It looks like he's on *my* trail now,' he said. 'I still can't figure out what made him think I might be here.'

Donovan was fuming. 'I've had a good hideout here in Brody,' he said. 'The last thing I want is for Madison to be nosing around. We've got to get rid of him as soon as we can.'

Peary agreed, and they spent some time working on and agreeing a plan to remove the danger to them caused by Jake's presence in Brody.

Late in the afternoon, Donovan made an excuse to call in at the livery stable, and he noted which stall contained Jake's horse. Then a few casual questions brought him the answers he wanted to hear. The liveryman and the hotel owner would, as Donovan knew they frequently did, be taking part in a game of poker late that evening in the saloon. He returned to the shack.

At eleven o'clock in the evening, Donovan and Peary left the shack. The street was dark and deserted. They walked past the store, and on towards the hotel. Between the buildings was a narrow alley, in which Peary concealed himself. Donovan walked on to the hotel and went inside. The lobby was deserted. He checked the register for Jake's room number, and saw that the corresponding key was missing from its hook. He went up the stairs and knocked on Jake's door. Jake, not yet in bed, opened it.

'I've come from the store,' said Donovan. 'Mr Newman asked me to tell you he'd like to see you there right now. Said to say he's just got some news about the man you were looking for.'

'Tell him I'll be along in a few minutes,' said Jake, and Donovan departed.

When Jake left the hotel, the street outside was deserted. He walked along it towards the store. As he passed the end of the narrow alley between the buildings, Donovan ran out silently behind him, and struck him hard on the back of the head with his six-gun. As Jake collapsed, Peary came out, and helped Donovan drag Jake into the alley. There, he was gagged and his hands were tied.

The two men then dragged their victim through the alley, and along the rear of the buildings to the shack. They took him inside. He was conscious now, and they bound him more tightly, and laid him on the floor. Then Donovan left the shack, and returned to the hotel. He entered Jake's room, using the key he had taken from his prisoner's pocket. He took all Jake's possessions from his room, and walked back with them to the shack.

'I've had an idea,' said Peary. 'We can't risk a shot being heard. You know that big empty timber chest standing outside, where the horses are. For the time being, let's tie Madison up real tight, drop him in there, and fasten the padlock that stops the top being lifted. He can lie in there, fretting about what's going to happen to him.'

'A good idea,' said Donovan, 'so long as we gag him proper, and tie him so tight he can't move. Let's do it now, but we'd better be quick.'

When they considered that their prisoner had been properly bound and gagged, they dragged him into the enclosure, and lowered him into the chest. It was a tight fit. They went back inside the shack, and quickly examined all Jake's belongings. They divided the roll of banknotes between them, then dropped all the remaining items into the chest, on top of Jake. Last of all they secured the heavy lid of the strongly built chest with the padlock.

'Tomorrow,' said Donovan after the two men had returned to the shack, 'I'll get a spade from somewhere, and we'll dig a hole in the enclosure for Madison's body. Then we'll shoot him dead while he's still in the chest. We'll rig up something to muffle the shot, so that it won't be noticed. But right now, I've got to get his horse. You saddle yours while I'm gone. I'll be back soon.'

Donovan went to the stable, aware that the poker game in the saloon would last for at least another half-hour. He went inside. It was dimly lit by one oil lamp. Quickly, he saddled Jake's horse and, unobserved, he led it out through the rear door of the stable, and along to the shack. A few minutes later Peary rode out of town on his own horse, leading Jake's mount. He returned well before dawn, disturbing Donovan, who was asleep in the shack.

'I turned Madison's horse loose two hours' ride south of here,' he said.

'Good,' said Donovan. 'I'll go out later to see

what talk there is about Madison leaving town during the night. And I'll bring a spade back with me.'

Outside the shack, imprisoned in the chest, Jake was suffering. His head was still aching from the blow delivered by Donovan, and he was so tightly bound that he could scarcely move his limbs. In the shack, he had recognized Peary, and he guessed that the man with him was Donovan. He strongly suspected that his own death was likely to be imminent.

Just before noon Donovan went to the saloon. The barkeep told him that the talk was that the stranger Madison had apparently ridden off during the night without telling anybody, and owing money. Satisfied, Donovan finished his drink, then walked out of the saloon. As he passed through the two swing doors and turned to walk along the boardwalk he instantly recognized the US deputy marshal walking towards him. He was a man called Holt, who had been a lawman in Arizona. Holt had known Donovan before the outlaw took to crime.

Holt's recognition of Donovan was fractionally delayed, and this spelt his doom. Donovan pulled from under his belt the six-gun concealed under his jacket, and shot Holt through the heart before the deputy could fire his own gun. The only witness to the shooting was a young boy sitting on the edge of the boardwalk on the other side of the street. Donovan ran along the side of the saloon, then behind the buildings to the shack. Rushing inside, he shouted to Peary that he had just killed a deputy US marshal, and they both needed to leave town immediately. Hurriedly they saddled their horses, and collected a few belongings.

Donovan was the first to ride off. Peary ran over to the chest, with the intention of lifting the lid and shooting Jake through the head. Then he remembered that the key to the padlock was in Donovan's pocket. At the same time, he heard the sound of raised voices along the street. Cursing, he hurriedly mounted his horse, and raced after Donovan. By the time the townspeople discovered, from the only witness of the shooting, that the man calling himself Fox was the one who had killed the deputy, Donovan and Peary were both out of sight. It later became clear that Holt had had no particular business in Brody. He was just passing through.

From inside the chest Jake heard, faintly, the sounds of the hurried departure of the two outlaws. Then there was silence. The midday sun was beating down on the chest, and the heat inside was almost unbearable. He was unable to move or call out. Without food, and particularly water, he wondered how long he could survive.

At the store, the Newmans were puzzled over

Jake's disappearance during the night. They were convinced that if he had been leaving of his own accord, he would have let them know. And when they heard that Fox had disappeared after killing a deputy US marshal, they wondered if he had been involved in Jake's disappearance. But it was all conjecture. They had no proof.

Three days after Holt was shot dead two deputy US marshals arrived in Brody to investigate the killing. The Newmans told them about Jake's disappearance, shortly after arriving in town in search of Bart Peary. After speaking to other towns-people, looking inside the shack which Holt's killer had occupied, and glancing into the enclosure where the chest was standing, the deputies left town.

SEVEN

Three days after the two deputy marshals left Brody, a cowboy called Fletcher, who worked on a cattle ranch in the Texas Panhandle, rode into Brody from the south, in the late afternoon. He had been given time off to visit his parents in Kansas. He was leading the horse, still saddled, on which Jake had arrived in Brody. Ellen Newman, walking along the boardwalk, recognized the horse, and stopped Fletcher. She told him about Jake's disappearance, asked him where he had found the horse, and whether he knew what had happened to its rider.

'Found it grazing about ten miles south of here,' said Fletcher. 'I figured maybe the rider had been thrown and hurt, but I searched the area for a while, and there was no sign of him. So I brought the horse along here to see if anybody knew the owner.'

'The owner's a good friend of me and my

husband,' said Ellen, 'and we owe him a lot. We run the general store along the street there. Tie the horse there, and my husband will tend to it.'

'Right,' said Fletcher. 'I'll do that. And I'll be on my way in the morning.'

When Ellen told her husband about the discovery of Jake's horse, he went to find Fletcher, who gave him the location of the spot where the animal had been found. On the following morning he rode out there with two friends from in town, and they searched the surrounding area for several hours for any sign of the missing man. But the search proved fruitless, and they returned to Brody.

The following morning, Ellen and her husband were in the store discussing the mystery of Jake's disappearance.

'I was thinking about it during the night,' said Ellen, 'and it struck me that maybe Fox's real name was Donovan, and maybe Peary had been staying in the shack with him. Perhaps they captured Jake and held him in the shack for a while, and took his horse from the stable. Maybe we should take a look inside the shack for clues that might tell us what happened to Jake.'

'No reason why not,' said her husband, 'though I saw the two deputies go in there. Things are pretty quiet in the store just now. Let's close it for half an hour, and take a look for ourselves.'

As they left the store, the blacksmith called to Newman from the other side of the street. The storekeeper told his wife to carry on to the shack while he found out what the blacksmith wanted. He said he would join her there in a few minutes.

Ellen walked on to the shack, and looked inside the enclosure where Fox had kept his horse. She realized that Peary's mount could also have been hidden there. She sat down on the chest to await the arrival of her husband.

Inside the chest, Jake's condition was serious. He was weak and in great discomfort from the prolonged lack of food and drink and the inability to move his limbs. He heard a slight creak from the lid of the chest as Ellen sat on it, and sensed that somebody was close by. Still gagged, he made a supreme effort which completely drained what little energy he had left, and managed a feeble tap on the side of the chest with the heel of his boot.

Ellen felt the slight vibration and heard the faint sound caused by the tap. She stood up just as her husband appeared in view.

'Mark!' she shouted. 'Something just moved inside this chest. I'm sure of it.'

Newman looked at the padlock, then ran back to the blacksmith, who returned to the shack with him, carrying a hammer and chisel. The lid was soon lifted, Jake's belongings were removed, then Jake himself was lifted out and laid on the ground.

'He don't look so good,' said Newman. 'Untie him and take the gag off while I go for Doc Chandler.'

When he returned with the doctor, Jake was still lying on the ground, with the gag and rope removed. Chandler checked him over.

'Don't know how much longer you'd have lasted in there,' he said, when he had finished, 'but now that you're out, and start eating and drinking the way I tell you to, you'll soon be back to normal.'

'Thanks, Doc,' said Jake, 'As soon as I can get my legs working again, I'll go and get a room at the hotel.'

'You'll do no such thing,' said Ellen. 'We've got a spare room. You can stay in there till you're fit.'

'I'm obliged,' said Jake. A little later, after he had told them how Peary and Donovan, alias Fox, had captured him and left him in the chest, he walked back to the store with the Newmans.

While recovering there he considered his next move in his effort to bring Bart Peary to justice. He had no idea where Peary and Donovan had gone when they left Brody. He decided that, before continuing his quest, he would ride back to Pueblo, to see how Billy was faring.

He left Brody a week after his rescue from the chest and after thanking the Newmans for the action which had probably saved his life. When he rode into Pueblo he called first at the laundry to see Mrs Ramsey. Billy was at school with her own children. Jake asked how the boy was doing.

'Still missing his parents,' she replied, 'but he talks a lot about you.'

Jake explained that he had not yet been able to hand Peary over to the law, and might not be in Pueblo long. He asked her to get Billy to come and see him at the hotel when he had finished school.

Billy came to Jake's hotel room an hour later. Jake told him what had happened in Brody, and said that as soon as he got any idea of where Peary might be, he would be on his trail again. Meanwhile, Billy would stay with Mrs Ramsey.

'After you've caught him,' asked Billy, 'are you going to be a lawman again? Where are we going to live?'

'Right now, Billy,' said Jake, 'I don't feel like going back to being a lawman. I have a hankering to run a small cattle ranch like my father did. Would you like to help me run a place like that, Billy?'

'I guess so,' the boy replied. 'That's what Pa was aiming to do if he could save enough money. But will I be able to go to school?'

'I'll make sure of that,' said Jake. 'I hope it ain't going to be long before we can start looking for a place. I'm going to see the sheriff in the morning. Maybe he has some news of Peary.'

In the morning Jake went to the sheriff's office.

He told Grant about events in Brody.

'So Bart Peary is on the loose,' he said, 'probably with a man called Donovan. I don't know where they are. Don't suppose you've heard anything about either of them?'

'No I haven't,' said Grant. 'What're you planning to do now?'

I'll stay here for a short while,' Jake replied. 'Maybe news'll come in about some robbery they've carried out.'

'If it does, I'll let you know,' said the sheriff.

When Peary and Donovan fled from Brody they headed for a hideout in an area, well known to Peary, north of Pueblo. On the way there they picked up an outlaw called Barton, well known to both of them. The intention was to form a criminal gang of three, with Peary as the leader. The hideout, for the time being, was to be in a small secluded ravine, well off the main trails. In the ravine some shelter was afforded by an old, long-abandoned shack.

They were not short of money. They still had most of the proceeds from their last robberies. They spent a week of rest and relaxation in the ravine. At the end of this week it became necessary to replenish their provisions. Barton, not as well known to the law as his two companions, rode into Pueblo for this purpose. When he returned, he had news for Peary and Donovan.

In the saloon he had heard the barkeep, who was related to Mrs Ramsey, telling another customer about Jake's return to Pueblo, and his intention of continuing the search for Peary, who had killed his wife in Wildern while robbing the bank. Barton also learnt that Jake was adopting Billy Denny, son of the settler Martha Denny, who had also been killed by Peary.

Peary remembered shooting towards a man and a woman as he was running from the bank in Wildern. He now knew that the woman must have been Madison's wife. He cursed.

'Damn Madison!' he said. 'Before we do anything else, we've got to get rid of him. But not in Pueblo. That'd be too risky. Somehow, we've got to get him to ride out of town, alone.'

They spent the next half-hour deciding on a plan which would rid them of Jake once and for all. Before the plan could be carried out, one or two further visits to Pueblo by Barton would be required, to collect certain information necessary for the success of the plan.

Three days after Barton's first visit to Pueblo, Jake was in his room at the hotel. It was mid-afternoon. He was expecting Billy to come and see him shortly for a chat, as he had done for the last few days, after school. But there was still no sign of the boy half an hour after the usual time of his arrival. Jake decided to go and see if Billy was at the laundry. As he descended the stairs into the lobby, he saw Darby, the hotel owner, coming towards him, holding an envelope which he handed to Jake as they met.

'Just found this on the desk,' he said. 'It's addressed to you. Don't know when it was left. I ain't been in the lobby during the last half-hour or so.'

As Jake was opening the envelope Darby turned and left him. Jake took the sheet of paper from the envelope, unfolded it, and read the words roughly scrawled on it in large capital letters. Badly shocked, he turned and went back to his room. He sat on a chair and looked at the message again. It read: I HAVE BILLY DENNY. BRING THE LAW IN AND THE BOY DIES. IT'S YOU I WANT MADISON. RIDE ALONE TOMORROW TO SIGNAL BUTTE ARRIVING NOON. WHEN WE HAVE YOU PRISONER THE BOY WILL BE FREED OUTSIDE PUEBLO. THE TOWN IS BEING WATCHED. FOLLOW THESE INSTRUCTIONS EXACTLY OR THE BOY DIES. BART PEARY.

Jake left the room and hurried to the laundry. He asked Mrs Ramsey if Billy was around.

'No,' she replied. 'I haven't seen him since school closed. Figured he was with you.'

Jake showed her the message he had just received.

'This is between us,' he said. 'Nobody else must know except us two. Billy's life may depend on it. Will you see if your two children noticed what Billy did when he left school?'

Mrs Ramsey, deeply concerned by what she had just read, went outside to speak to her two children. When she returned she told Jake that her boy had noticed a stranger speaking to Billy just after he left school, but he hadn't seen where Billy went after that.

'I've got no choice,' said Jake. I'll do exactly as they say. I'm sure Peary's aiming to kill me, but maybe I can turn the tables somehow. For the time being we've got to keep the kidnapping secret. How do we do that, I wonder?'

'He won't be missed at school for the next two days,' said Mrs Ramsey. 'It's closed. And I'll tell my boy and girl that Billy's staying with you for a spell.'

'That should do it,' said Jake. 'D'you happen to know where Signal Butte is?'

'I've heard of it,' she said, 'but I've never been there. They say it can be seen for miles from any direction. I think it's north and west of here. I'm not sure how far away it is, but there's a map in the schoolhouse that'll show you exactly where it's located. Go and take a look. The teacher usually stays on a while after the children have left.'

'I'll do that,' said Jake. 'And I can't be sure, but I'm hoping that Peary will keep his promise, and that not long after I reach Signal Butte tomorrow, Billy will be turning up here.'

'I sure hope so,' said Mrs Ramsey, 'and I'm hoping to see you not long after that.'

But even as she spoke, she thought it most unlikely that she would ever see Jake again.

Jake left town the following morning, after telling the liveryman he was taking a ride through the surrounding area. Long before he reached Signal Butte he could see, in the distance, the high, isolated, steep-sided hill which was his destination. He scanned the whole area in front of him. There was no one in sight.

He rode on towards the butte, and as he neared the foot, around noon, two men stepped out from behind a large boulder standing at the foot of the slope. Each man was holding a gun, which was trained on Jake as he rode slowly up to them and stopped. He immediately recognized the two as Peary and Donovan. Peary ordered Jake to dismount, and Donovan took his six-gun and rifle, and checked him for additional weapons. Peary regarded the captive with grim satisfaction.

'You made a big mistake, Madison,' he said, 'when you set out to follow me and hand me over to the law. You were lucky not to die in Brody. This time it'll be different. I could shoot you through the head right now, and that would be the end of it. But we thought about that a lot, and we reckon it'd be too easy for you. So we've figured out a way for you to die which is going to take a whole lot longer than that.'

'You'll let the boy go now?' asked Jake.

Peary grinned evilly. 'Don't be a fool, Madison,' he said. 'We can't have him blabbing to the law about us and the hideout we use near here. Our partner's holding him there right now. We reckon to keep him with us to do all our chores. And who knows, when he's a bit older, maybe we can make a robber out of him.'

Jake's face showed no emotion, but even on such a short acquaintance, he had taken a great liking to Billy, and inside, he was seething with anger and frustration. If the slightest opportunity of escaping arose, he was determined to seize it.

Jake was ordered to mount, then his hands were tied behind him. With Donovan leading Jake's horse, they rode off to the west, towards the Rocky Mountains, visible in the distance. After riding for an hour, they came to a steep-sided flat-topped hill, and stopped at the foot of the slope. In front of them Jake could see what looked like the entrance to a long-abandoned mine tunnel.

Jake was pulled out of the saddle, then Peary held a gun on him. Donovan lit an oil lamp he had been carrying, and Jake was ordered into the tunnel. With the two outlaws close behind him, he entered it and walked slowly through it. He could see that the walls were about six feet high, and the floor was about three feet wide. The roof was supported by stout pieces of timber, still apparently in reasonable condition. After about twenty yards, the tunnel came to an abrupt end, and they could see only a blank wall in front of them.

Jake was ordered to lie down, and Donovan trussed him with a length of rope which Peary handed him.

'This is goodbye, Madison,' said Peary. 'We'll be thinking about you in here over the next week or two.'

Laughing, the two outlaws walked back towards the entrance. They stopped when they were halfway there, and Peary took from his pocket two sticks of dynamite which had been purchased in Pueblo by Barton. He pushed one stick into a narrow gap above one of the roof-supporting timbers. Moving a few paces towards the entrance, he inserted the second stick in a similar position. Then he lit the two fuse-cords, both long enough to give him and Donovan time to leave the tunnel before the explosions occurred. As they watched in safety, they heard the sounds of the explosions, and saw the cloud of dust billowing from the entrance to the tunnel.

Inside the tunnel, Jake heard the ear-splitting

sounds of the two explosions, and went into a paroxysm of coughing as the dust enveloped him. He continued coughing for some time after the dust had settled.

The two outlaws waited a short while, then entered the tunnel with the lamp, and walked cautiously along it. When they came near to the point where the dynamite had been placed they could see that the tunnel was completely blocked by a roof-fall.

'Nobody could dig another tunnel through that without supporting the roof,' said Peary. 'Madison sure won't be bothering us no more. Let's go and join up with Barton and the boy at the hideout.'

When Jake's fit of coughing had abated, he realized the gravity of the situation. Although uninjured by the explosions, he was tightly bound, was in complete darkness, and the tunnel between him and the entrance was almost certainly blocked. It was clear that the first thing he needed to do was to try and free himself.

He wriggled around on the floor of the tunnel until he was lying on his side, with his back against the wall. Moving slowly along the bottom of the wall, he felt with his fingers for the sharp edge of a piece of projecting rock. Laboriously inching his way along, it was not until he had almost reached the blockage that he felt a sharp edge which projected sufficiently for his purpose.

He placed the rope holding his wrists together against the sharp edge, and moved the rope back and forth. Progress was very slow. The rope kept slipping off the edge, and the strain on his arms and shoulders was almost unbearable. He had to take frequent rests, and he lost all count of time. When the rope parted at last he rested a while before removing it from the upper part of his body and freeing his legs.

When, eventually, he was able to stand up he moved forward with his hands outstretched until he felt the blockage. He soon established that the fall had completely blocked the tunnel. He reached up to ceiling height, and removed some of the material which had fallen down. But this triggered another fall, and he stepped back just in time to avoid being hit. After several other unsuccessful attempts to open up a passage through the blockage, he realized that it was futile to continue. He sat on the floor, with his back to the wall, staring into the blackness, wondering how long he could survive without water, food and fresh air.

EIGHT

Seven days after Jake was imprisoned in the tunnel, wandering prospector Hank Logan was riding his mule past the hill in which Jake was entombed. A burro trailed behind him. He spotted the tunnel entrance, turned, and rode up to it. Logan, a lean, grizzled man in his sixties, had been prospecting in California and Nevada for many years, without any notable success. He had recently decided to continue his search in Colorado for the elusive find that would make him rich.

He dismounted and took a lamp and a small pick from the burro. He lit the lamp and walked into the tunnel. As he did so he noticed, on a patch of soft, bare ground, recent footprints leading in and out of the tunnel. He walked along it until he reached the blockage, which looked to him as though it had been caused by a recent fall.

He placed the lamp on the ground and, using the small pick, he knocked out a piece of rock projecting from the wall. He examined it closely, then threw it down. He knocked two further pieces of rock out, examined and discarded them. He bent down to pick up the lamp. As he straightened up, about to leave, he froze. He heard a tapping sound, almost inaudible, which appeared to be coming from the far side of the fall.

He waited until the tapping ceased. Then, with the point of his pick he struck, three times, a large piece of rock embedded in the wall. Seconds later, he heard three faint taps in reply. He struck the same piece of rock five times, and heard five taps in reply. There seemed to be no doubt that some-body was trapped on the far side of the fall.

With his mining experience Logan knew that he needed help, as well as a supply of timber, to make a safe passage through the fall. He decided to ride back to the small town of Tasco, six miles to the north, where he had spent the night. As he walked out of the tunnel he took a good look at the foot-prints outside. He had experience of tracking, and close examination showed him that, not long ago, two people had gone in and out of the tunnel twice, while a third had gone in and had not left.

When he reached Tasco he first went to the store, where he told the storekeeper, Kilroy, what he had seen and heard in the tunnel, and what was needed to effect a rescue.

'There's some timber out back,' said Kilroy. 'You

go and pick what you need. Meanwhile, I'll collect two friends of mine, and the three of us will go to the tunnel with you. My wife will look after the store.'

Thirty-five minutes later a large buckboard, carrying the timber, the three townsmen, and other items required, left town. Logan rode alongside. When they reached the tunnel they all went inside with lamps, and walked up to the fall. Logan called for silence, then struck the wall three times with his pick. Moments later, they heard three faint taps in reply.

With the help of the others Logan placed new supports for the roof near the fall. Then they started digging out a tunnel, smaller than the previous one, supporting the roof and sides as they went along. Progress was slow, and it was three hours past midnight before they broke through into the area where Jake had been imprisoned. Logan called out to him.

'You reckon you can crawl out through here?' he asked.

'I guess so,' Jake replied weakly, and entered the tunnel, crawling slowly along it as Logan retreated. They helped him out at the far end, and sat him against the wall. He was handed a canteen of water, from which he drank sparingly, before speaking to his audience.

'I'm obliged to you folks,' he said. 'I don't

reckon I'd have lasted much longer in there. The air was getting pretty foul.'

'How long since the roof came down?' asked Kilroy.

'I ain't got no idea,' Jake replied. 'What's the date today?'

When Kilroy gave it to him, Jake told them he had been in the tunnel for a week. He went on to tell them how he came to be there, and Kilroy told him, quickly, how Logan had organized his rescue.

'We'd better get you back to Tasco on the buckboard,' he said. 'You'll need to eat. My wife'll whip up something for you when we get there. Then you can rest up at the hotel for a few days. I'll get the doctor to call in there to see you. You still aiming to carry on looking for this outlaw Peary?'

'I am,' Jake replied. 'I've got more reason than ever now. I've got to get Billy back.'

Jake recovered quickly over the next few days. He went to see the banker in town, who supplied him with the money to cover living expenses and to pay for a horse and saddle, weapons and ammunition. Three days after Jake had been rescued Logan rode into town and came to see how he was faring. Jake told him that he was aiming to ride to Pueblo the following day and would probably stay a while at the hotel there, in the hope that the sheriff would get some information about the whereabouts of Peary and the others.

'I sure hope you manage to catch up with the gang and free the boy,' said Logan. 'Myself, I'm figuring to take a look at Wyoming Territory. I'm heading straight there. Should cross the border in seven or eight days.'

Once again, Jake thanked the prospector, who started to leave, then turned back.

'Who knows?' he said. 'Maybe I might meet up with them varmints myself. What do they look like?'

After Jake had described Peary and Donovan, and also Billy, Logan departed.

The following morning Jake left Tasco and headed for Pueblo. On reaching the town his first call was at the sheriff's office. Grant was inside. Jake had already sent him a message from Tasco, telling him of events at Signal Butte and the tunnel. He asked Grant if there had been any news of the whereabouts of Peary and the others.

'Not a word,' said the sheriff. 'I can tell you, everybody here is mighty upset about them taking the boy. What I've done since I got your message, is ask law officers in surrounding states and territories to watch out for the Peary gang and the boy. If they are sighted, I'll be told right away. So far, I've heard nothing.'

'I'll stay in Pueblo for the time being,' said Jake, 'in case any information comes through. I'm real worried about the boy, but I can't think of anything else I can do.'

'All right,' said Grant. 'Any news I get, I'll pass on to you right away. Have you seen Mrs Ramsey yet? I told her what happened to you after you left Pueblo. She keeps asking about the boy.'

'I'm going along there now,' said Jake.

He found Mrs Ramsey in the laundry, and explained that he was waiting in Pueblo for news of Billy's whereabouts, before starting out on any rescue attempt. He could see that, like himself, she was deeply concerned about Billy's welfare.

Eleven days passed without news of the Peary gang and Billy, and Jake was growing more and more concerned. Then, late on the twelfth day, he received a telegraph message from an unexpected source. It was addressed to him, at the hotel. It read: SPOTTED GANG AND BOY HIDING IN CAVE IN RAVINE EIGHT MILES NORTH OF STONY CREEK WYOMING. GET HERE QUICK AS YOU CAN. SUGGEST STAGECOACH TO CHEYENNE. SEE BLACKSMITH WHEN YOU ARRIVE STONY CREEK. HE WILL KNOW WHERE I AM. HANK LOGAN.

Jake took the message to the sheriff's office, and showed it to Grant.

'I know where Stony Creek is,' he told the sheriff. 'It's not far north-west of Cheyenne. I'll take the first stage. That'll be in the morning.'

'D'you want me to send any message to the

102

county sheriff in Wyoming?' asked Grant.

'No,' replied Jake. 'I don't want to risk any harm coming to Billy. I'll get in touch with the sheriff there when the time is right.'

Jake took the stage the following morning, and reached Cheyenne the day after that. He hired a horse at the livery stable and rode to Stony Creek. It was dark when he arrived. It was a small town, with a single street. He located the blacksmith's shop, and stopped outside. The big door was closed, but there was a light inside. Jake knocked hard on the door, which was opened by Emery the blacksmith.

Jake introduced himself, and asked the black-smith whether Hank Logan had left a message for him. Before replying, Emery beckoned Jake inside and closed the door behind him.

'I have bad news for you,' he said. 'Logan is dead. He was found south of town yesterday, with head wounds. He was lying on the ground, with his mule and burro close by. Nobody knows how he came by those wounds. When I saw him last he said he might be leaving a message for you when the time came, but it looks like he died before he could do that.

'I do the undertaker's job around here. I built a coffin for Logan, and we buried him in the grave-yard this afternoon.'

Shocked by the news, Jake felt sure that Logan

had been killed by the Peary gang, who must have found out that he was spying on them at the hideout. He decided to take Emery into his confidence, and told him about his pursuit of Peary, and the kidnapping of Billy. He showed him the telegraph message he had received from Logan, and asked him if he knew of the ravine and cave mentioned.

'Yes, I've seen a ravine eight miles north of here,' Emery replied. 'That must be the one. It's well away from any of the trails, and there's a strong flow of water through it. I didn't see the cave, but I weren't that close. It would be a good place for a hideout, I reckon. If you ride due north from here, you can't miss it.'

'I'm hoping they're still there,' said Jake. 'I'll take a meal in town, then ride out there during the night, and find a place where I can hide, and watch the cave. If I find out that they *are* there, I'll have to think up some way of rescuing the boy without him being harmed.'

Jake left Stony Creek a little before midnight and kept the North Star straight ahead of him. He had no difficulty in locating the ravine, which ran across his path. As he neared it he could plainly hear the sound of rushing water. He swung left and rode up to the head of the ravine, to a point from which he could look down along it. He decided to sit there for a short while, straining his eyes and ears for any indication of the presence of the gang.

Just as he was about to rise to his feet to start a closer investigation down inside the ravine, he saw the sudden spurt of flame from a match being struck to light a cigarette. The location of the smoker was about halfway down the south side of the ravine, about seventy yards from Jake. He guessed that there was a night guard stationed at the entrance to the cave.

He rode back to a grove of trees, half a mile from the ravine, which he had noticed earlier, and tethered his horse inside it. Then he returned to the ravine, and climbed down the slope on the south side at a point well downstream from the place where the match had been lit. Halfway down he came to a ledge, several yards wide, which appeared to run up and down the ravine. Below the ledge was a sheer drop to the fast-flowing water below.

He looked round for a place where he could hide, and from which he should be able to see the cave entrance when daylight came. He soon found a sizeable patch of brush which would suit his purpose. It was located at the foot of the sloping side of the ravine, where it met the ledge. He made a passage through the brush to the centre, closing it behind him as he moved along. He settled down there to await the dawn.

When daylight came he stood up and cautiously

parted the top of the brush to allow him to look along the ledge towards the cave. A man was standing outside it. Jake was almost certain that the man was Donovan, presumably on guard at the cave entrance. As he watched the man turned and looked down the ravine for a short while. Jake was now sure, beyond doubt, that he was looking at Donovan. The question now was how to rescue Billy.

Just under half an hour later he was still wrestling with this problem, while watching the cave entrance, when he saw Billy run out of the cave, with Peary in hot pursuit. The outlaw grabbed Billy's arm and started hitting him hard and continuously around the head. Desperate to escape the onslaught, Billy wrenched himself free, and ran from his attacker. But he had forgotten how close he was to the edge of the ledge. Before he could stop himself he was falling towards the fast-running water below. Jake saw him disappear over the edge. He forced his way out of the brush, ran across the ledge, and dropped into the water himself. He hit it a few yards downstream of Billy, and sank below the surface. When he reappeared he saw Billy, choking and panic-stricken, close by. He grabbed him, and supported him as they were carried swiftly downstream.

Both Donovan and Peary saw Jake leave his hiding-place and disappear. They ran to the top of the sheer wall rising from the water, and saw Jake and Billy floating quickly away from them. They both fired their six-guns at the man and boy in the water until they disappeared out of sight round a slight bend in the ravine. During the firing they were joined by Barton who came from inside the cave.

'Did that look like Madison to you?' Donovan asked Peary.

'He was about the same build,' Peary replied, 'but how in hell could Madison have got loose? Get the horses out of the cave. We've got to follow them down the ravine and finish them both off, if they ain't already drowned.'

Jake heard the bullets from the outlaws' guns hitting the water close by, but he and the boy floated round the bend unscathed. A little way ahead of them Jake spotted a recess in the wall of the ravine, just above water level, where part of the rock face had broken away. Still supporting Billy, he swam up to it and, shortly after, both he and Billy were standing in the recess, clear of the water, and out of view of anyone on the ledge above. Jake looked at the angry bruises on Billy's face.

'Are you all right, Billy?' he asked.

Billy nodded. He seemed to be recovering from his fall and his immersion in the cold water.

'We'll stay here for a while, Billy,' said Jake, who had just noticed that his six-gun had disappeared from its holster while he was in the water. 'Those three will be riding down the ravine after us any minute. And when they can't find us soon, I figure they'll ride back to the cave for anything they've left there. Then they'll leave the area.'

Jake was absolutely right. Having ridden two miles downstream without seeing any sign of Jake and Billy, Peary paused to consider the situation. He was now certain that the man with Billy was Madison. How many other people, he wondered, apart from Madison and the old prospector, were aware that the gang was hiding in the cave? They could waste no more time on the search. They must collect their things and leave the area as quickly as possible.

Jake and Billy heard the three men riding along the hard surface of the ledge above them. Less than an hour elapsed before they heard them return to the cave. Twenty minutes later they heard them passing once again. Jake waited half an hour, then he and Billy re-entered the water and floated down to a spot where part of the ledge had fallen away, leaving a slope which they climbed up, to reach the remainder of the ledge above. Then they walked along to the cave, and went inside. It had obviously been vacated by the gang.

'I think we're safe now, Billy,' said Jake. 'The sun's pretty warm. I reckon we should strip down and dry our clothes. Then we'll pick up my horse and ride to Stony Creek.'

They reached the town around noon, and rode up to the blacksmith's shop. Emery came out as they were dismounting. He looked at Billy, then turned to Jake.

'I see you got part of the job done,' he said. 'How about the rest?'

Jake told him what had happened. He said that he was sending Billy back to Pueblo by stagecoach, then he would try and follow the trail of the gang.

'You've got time to ride to Cheyenne and catch today's coach,' said Emery.

'Good,' said Jake. 'The sooner I can start out after those three, the better. Trouble is, I ain't that good at tracking. You wouldn't know anybody around here I could hire to help me follow the trail of Peary and the others?'

'Maybe I *can* help with that,' said Emery. 'I have a cousin called Abe Kennedy. He served a long time as an Army scout, and a good one, by all accounts. He learnt the skills from a Pawnee scout he worked alongside. He retired a couple of months ago, and settled down in Cheyenne. Rides here to see me now and then. I get the feeling he's finding life a mite boring. I reckon he might be glad to help you. Go and see him when you get to Cheyenne.'

When Jake and Billy reached Cheyenne they talked while waiting for the stagecoach. Billy told how he had been forced to do all the chores, and had been regularly beaten by Peary. Then he pleaded with Jake.

'I don't want to leave you,' he said. 'Let me come with you. I can help you to catch those men.'

'Well, it's like this, Billy,' said Jake. 'You're just a mite young to be chasing after killers like Peary. I can work better if I know you're safe in Pueblo. And if I do find them, I aim to call in the law to help me. What I'd like you to do is give a message to Sheriff Grant in Pueblo, and stay with Mrs Ramsey till I come for you.'

Jake told Billy what to say to the sheriff, finishing just as the coach was ready to board. Billy climbed in, and Jake asked the driver to watch out for the boy, and to pass on the request to any driver taking over. When the coach had left Jake went to Kennedy's house, following directions given him by Emery. Kennedy answered his knock and invited him inside. He was a man of medium height, sturdy and clean-shaven, with a light step and a keen eye, despite his sixty-one years.

Jake introduced himself, and said he had just come from Kennedy's cousin in Stony Creek. He told Kennedy of the day's events, and the reasons for his presence in the area. Kennedy listened with interest.

'I aim to follow the gang just as soon as I can,' said Jake, 'but I ain't much of a tracker. I was wondering if I could hire you to lend me a hand.'

'To tell the truth,' said Kennedy, 'I'll be glad of something to do. I ain't used to being so idle. There's no time to lose. We'll leave here before dawn for the cave where the boy was held.'

'I'm obliged,' said Jake. 'I'm going to buy myself a six-gun now, then I'll take a room at the hotel. I could sure do with some sleep. I'll call for you here before dawn.'

The following morning, when they reached the cave, Jake stayed there while Kennedy took a look at the tracks left by the three outlaws when they abandoned the cave the previous day. When he returned to Jake, he told him that Peary and the others were heading south towards the border with Colorado.

They followed the tracks across the border, Jake marvelling at Kennedy's ability to read sign which was completely invisible or unintelligible to himself. They found the place where the three men had camped overnight, and stayed there themselves till morning. Then they continued to follow the tracks. Late in the afternoon Kennedy told Jake that the tracks seemed to be heading straight for Denver. He was proved right when Denver came in sight, just as darkness was falling, and soon the tracks were lost among those of many other horses moving in and out of town.

'Well that's that,' said Jake. 'It looks like either

they're in Denver, or they called here and left. I think a word with Sheriff Cassidy might be a good idea.'

They found Cassidy in his office. The sheriff remembered Jake from his previous visit.

'I heard about you and the boy being captured by Bart Peary,' he said, 'and I heard you managed to escape. But what about the boy?'

Jake told him of recent events, and introduced Abe Kennedy. He asked the sheriff whether he thought Peary and the others might be in hiding in Denver.

'It's possible,' Cassidy replied. 'They may have friends in town, where they could stay in hiding. What's the name of the man who joined Peary and Donovan?'

'Billy told me he heard one of the others call him Barton,' said Jake.

'I know Barton,' said the sheriff. 'Not long ago he finished a spell in prison for robbery. Let me make a few enquiries around town to see if anybody's seen Peary or the others.'

'All right,' said Jake. 'We'll take a couple of rooms at the hotel.'

NINE

While Jake and Kennedy were in the sheriff's office in Denver, Donovan walked through the darkness along the boardwalk outside it, on his way to the store. He had never been face to face with Cassidy. He glanced through the window as he passed, and saw the two men sitting by the sheriff's desk. He was sure that one of them was Madison. Cursing, he walked on a few paces, then turned and retraced his steps. A quick glance through the window confirmed that he was right.

He crossed the street, and waited in the shadows until Jake and Abe left the office. He followed them until he saw them go into the hotel along the street. Then he abandoned his visit to the store, and hurried back to the Bonanza saloon. He climbed up some steps on the outside of the building, passed through a door, and went along a passage to a room where Peary and Barton were sitting with Bannister, the owner of the saloon.

Bannister was a prosperous-looking well-dressed man in his forties. He made big profits from running a crooked gambling operation in his saloon, and added to these by sheltering, at exorbitant rates, outlaws running from the law. Such guests were accommodated in rooms above the saloon, and their needs were attended to by a well-paid staff who could be relied on not to divulge the identities of Bannister's criminal guests.

Donovan told Peary and Barton that he had seen Madison and another man in the sheriff's office, and that they were now in the hotel.

'So much for the time we spent hiding our tracks between here and Wyoming Territory,' said Peary. 'I wonder who Madison's partner is? We've got to get rid of them once and for all.'

He turned to Bannister, and asked him if Raven and his two associates, Morse and Porter were in town. The three men referred to, led by Raven, were professional assassins, willing to hunt down and kill almost anybody if the money was right. Their services did not come cheap, but it was said that they had never failed to complete a mission. Although suspected by the law of criminal activities, there had never been sufficient evidence to convict them.

'They're in town,' said Bannister. 'I saw them this morning.'

'I reckon us three should stay inside for the time

being,' said Peary. 'Would you ask Raven to come and see us about a job we'd like him to do?'

'I'll do that,' said Bannister. 'I think I know where to find him.'

Bannister returned with Raven half an hour later. Raven was a tall, burly man, dressed in dark clothing, with a bleak, pockmarked face. He listened impassively as Peary told of the relentless pursuit of himself by Madison since his wife had been killed, and of Madison's presence, with an unknown companion, in Denver.

'I'm getting mighty tired of him following me around,' said Peary, 'and I want you to kill the two of them.'

'It so happens we've nothing else on right now,' said Raven. 'So we'll take the job on if you agree our terms.'

'I don't see any problem with that,' said Peary. 'Will you do the job while they're here in town?'

'Too risky,' Raven replied. 'We like to work well away from towns, with no witnesses around. So the first thing is to lure Madison and his partner out of Denver.'

After giving a few minutes' consideration as to how this might be done, Raven asked Bannister if he happened to know a prospector working a claim ten miles or so south of Denver who might be bribed to report in town that he had seen the Peary gang not far from his claim.

'I know just the man,' said Bannister. 'He owes me some money for gambling debts, and I think he was in trouble with the law down in Texas before he came here. I'm sure he'll do what you want. His name's Garner. And it so happens I saw him in the saloon just before I came up here.'

'Good,' said Raven. 'The next thing is to make sure that the sheriff's out of town when Garner comes in with the news. I think I can arrange that. Otherwise he might organize a posse to join up with Madison and his partner when they set off after the Peary gang. And that's something we *don't* want to happen.'

Raven suggested to Bannister that the two of them should go down and talk with Garner in the saloon, if he was still there. Bannister checked that he was, then he and Raven talked with the prospector in Bannister's office behind the bar. The proposal put to him, and agreed, was that for an agreed sum of money he would ride into town when instructed, to say to a man called Madison at the hotel that he had heard he was looking for three outlaws. And he thought, from the descriptions he had been given, that he had seen them near his claim.

Raven told Garner that he would ride out to the claim early the following day to agree with him the spot at which he would say he saw the gang riding by. Then Garner would await Raven's instructions to ride into Denver to see Madison. Garner was not told about the presence of the Peary gang in town, nor was he given any reason for the passing of false information to Madison.

Early the following morning, Porter left Raven and Morse at the small house they had rented, and rode out of town to the north. He was a slim, bearded man of average height, with the same bleak, ruthless look about him as Raven. After six miles, he came to a point where the trail ran close to a stream for a short distance. He dismounted, and looked around. There was no one in sight. He looked up at the top of the telegraph pole beside which he was standing. The wire supported at the top of the pole was carrying telegraph messages into Denver from the north.

He opened the canvas sack he had been carrying, and took out a telegraph transmitting key and battery and a long metal spike. For the next twenty-five minutes or so his experience in a telegraph-line construction gang, before he joined Raven, would stand him in good stead.

He drove the spike into the bed of the stream to provide a ground connection. Then he climbed up the pole with the key and battery, cut the telegraph wire, and connected the key to the wire on the Denver side of the cut. When this had been done he keyed a message to the telegraph office in Denver. It was addressed to Sheriff Cassidy. It read:

WARREN GANG ROBBED BANK IN CHEYENNE EARLY TODAY. KILLED MANAGER, TELLER AND DEPUTY SHERIFF. ONE OF GANG CAPTURED. WARREN AND TWO OTHERS SEEN CROSSING COLORADO BORDER SOUTH OF CHEYENNE. REASON TO BELIEVE THEY ARE HEADING FOR HIDEOUT NOT FAR NORTH OF DENVER. CAN YOU INTERCEPT. COUNTY SHERIFF TURNER CHEYENNE.

When Porter had finished sending the message, he disconnected the key and returned to the ground. He did not repair the break, so preventing Cassidy from contacting the sheriff in Cheyenne for further information before leaving with the posse. He recovered the spike and rode back to Denver. Riding through the outskirts of town, he was passed by Sheriff Cassidy and five other riders, heading north.

As he rode up to the house he saw, riding towards him along the street, Raven, who had left town much earlier than himself to visit Garner. He waited, and they went into the house together. Porter told the others that he had sent the message, and that Cassidy had obviously taken the bait, since he had just led a posse out of town, riding north.

'Good,' said Raven. 'Everything's going fine. I've picked a good place for the ambush, and I've got Garner waiting just outside town. I'm going now to tell him to ride in to see Madison.'

Soon after receiving the telegraph message Sheriff Cassidy had paid a brief visit to Jake and Abe at the hotel. He told them that he was leaving with a posse in an attempt to capture the notorious Warren gang between Denver and the Colorado border. He said that no one had yet reported seeing the Peary gang in town or in the surrounding area.

Shortly after the posse had left, Jake and Abe went to the hotel dining room for breakfast. They had just finished the meal, and were preparing to leave, when Garner came into the room and approached them. He said he had some information which might interest them. Jake pointed to a vacant chair at the table, and Garner sat down.

'I heard you've been chasing the Peary gang,' he said, 'and I know the sheriff's been asking around whether anybody's seen them. Well, I reckon I saw them soon after dawn today, near my claim nine miles south of here. They were riding along the foot of a ridge running east to west. Then they rode into a gap in the ridge and headed south out of sight. So I rode in to tell the sheriff what I'd seen. But it seems he's heading north with a posse, after the Warren gang. So I figured I'd better come to you.'

'What made you think it was the Peary gang?' asked Jake.

'I weren't all that far away,' said Garner, 'and they seemed the right build. And one of them was riding a pinto.'

Jake had learnt from Billy that Barton was riding a pinto, and he had told the sheriff this.

'It looks like they *could* be the men we're after,' said Jake. 'We're obliged for the information. I reckon we'll ride out to that ridge right now, and see if we can pick up their trail. Maybe you could give us directions?'

'I'll do better than that,' said Garner. 'Give me forty minutes to tend to some business in town, and I'll take you to my claim. I can point the ridge out to you from there.'

'Thanks,' said Jake. 'We'll wait for you outside the livery stable.'

As Garner left the hotel he spoke to Raven, who was waiting outside. He told him that he would be leaving town with Madison and his partner forty minutes later.

Raven went for Porter and Morse, and the trio rode out of town shortly after. In due course they came in sight of the ridge of which Garner had spoken to Jake and Abe. Between them and the ridge were two rock outcrops running at right angles to the trail, which passed between them, and led on to the gap in the ridge. When they came closer to the outcrops, they divided. Raven rode to the eastern end of the outcrop to the left of the trail. Morse and Porter rode to the western end of the other outcrop. They concealed their horses behind the outcrops, climbed the slopes to the tops, and moved to positions over the trail where they could lie concealed. All three carried a Winchester 1873 model, with the extra rear sight for greater accuracy. Each one of them was an expert marksman. They settled down to wait.

Back in Denver, while waiting for Garner, Jake asked Abe if he was content to carry on helping in the search for the Peary gang.

'Sure,' said Abe. 'I'm enjoying it. If it happens I change my mind, I'll let you know.'

Garner joined them shortly after, and rode with them to his claim. He pointed out the ridge, and the gap into which he said he had seen the Peary gang ride.

'You see those two outcrops over there,' he said, pointing. 'The trail to the gap goes between them. I sure hope you manage to catch up with the gang.'

Jake thanked Garner, and he and Abe rode off to join the trail leading to the gap in the ridge. As they approached the outcrops Abe suddenly stopped. Jake followed suit.

'That's odd,' said Abe. 'I've been noticing the tracks of three horses on this trail, all pretty fresh, and I'm sure they weren't made by the Peary gang. And here where we've stopped, they separated. One set of tracks branches off to the left, the others to the right. I've got the same feeling I used to get in the Army, when something told me the Indians were about to attack. And I was usually right.

'These tracks are leading towards the only ends of the outcrops that look like they can be climbed. Maybe there are three riflemen up there, waiting to shoot us down as soon as we're in range. And another thing. Since Garner was so obliging as to ride into town to tell us what he'd seen, why didn't he take us right up to the ridge?'

'I wondered about that myself,' said Jake. 'Maybe Peary's set a trap for us. Maybe Garner's working for Peary. We'd better stay out of range of any rifle fire from those outcrops.'

They considered the situation, then Jake raised his arm and pointed ahead to the left, as if they were discussing a change of direction. They left the trail on their right, and headed for the ridge, along a path which was outside the range of rifle fire from the outcrops. When they reached the foot of the ridge, they turned, and rode slowly towards the gap, then into it. When they reached a point out of view of the outcrops they dismounted, climbed to the top of the ridge, and watched the outcrops from cover. They were just in time to see three men climbing down from them.

'So I was right,' said Abe. 'Who the devil can those three be?'

'Can't say,' said Jake. 'Whoever they are, we can't prove they were aiming to kill us. But I'm sure they were.'

As they watched, the three men went for their horses, which had been concealed at the feet of the outcrops, then joined up. They stood together for a while, then mounted, and rode slowly towards the gap in the ridge. Jake and Abe hurriedly rejoined their mounts, and rode off fast, to the far side of the ridge, then along the trail to the south. Soon it would be dark.

Raven cursed when he saw Jake and Abe leave the trail before they reached the trap which had been set for them. He could only guess that they had, for a reason he could not fathom, gone to look for tracks along the foot of the ridge, along which, they had been told by Garner, the Peary gang had ridden before passing through the gap. He waited twenty minutes after Jake and Abe had disappeared from view, then shouted to Morse and Porter to climb down, then join up with him below.

When they met up, a brief discussion followed,

during which they decided to ride on in pursuit of the two men who had recently disappeared through the gap, and to finish the job they had undertaken. They stopped just before reaching the gap, and waited till an hour after darkness had fallen. Then they proceeded cautiously through it to the other side of the ridge.

They continued south along the trail for seven miles, then they spotted the glow of a campfire ahead. They dismounted, tethered their horses, and cautiously advanced on the fire, through the darkness. Soon they were able to see what appeared to be two blanket-covered figures lying near the fire.

They stood watching them for a moment, then all three advanced closer to the fire. They stood side by side as they emptied their six-guns into the two figures lying on the ground. As the shooting started, Jake and Abe rose from a patch of brush in which they had been concealed, and crept up behind Raven and the others. As the last shots were being fired, Jake pistol-whipped Raven on the side of the head, and before Morse, standing by Raven's side, realized what was happening, he himself had received the same treatment from Jake. Abe pistol-whipped Porter at the same time as Jake dealt with Raven.

The three intruders collapsed on the ground. Their weapons were taken, and their hands were tied. Jake struck a match, and he and Abe looked at the faces of the three captives.

'I don't know them,' said Abe. 'How about you?'

'Me neither,' Jake replied. 'We'll take them back to Denver. Maybe somebody there'll know who they are. One thing's sure. If we'd ridden between those two outcrops, we wouldn't be alive now.'

One by one the three men lying on the ground stirred as they recovered consciousness. They stared up at the two men holding guns on them.

'Just stay where you are,' said Jake, 'and maybe you'd like to say who you are, and who sent you after us?'

This was a new situation for Raven and the others. Never before had the tables been turned on them so completely by their intended victims. They remained silent.

'I figured not,' said Jake. 'Maybe we'll find out more about you when we get you to Denver tomorrow.'

Abe went to look for the prisoners' horses, and returned with them shortly after. Then the captives' feet were tied, and the bundles of brush which had deceived them were taken from underneath the blankets. During the night, Abe and Jake took turns at guarding the prisoners.

They left for Denver after dawn, with the captives, hands tied behind them, riding their own horses. Keeping out of sight of Garner's claim, they arrived in Denver before noon, and the prisoners were led up to the sheriff's office. Sheriff Cassidy was still away with the posse, but there was a deputy sheriff called Ellison inside, who was well aware of the reason for the recent arrival in Denver, from Wyoming, of Jake and Abe.

Jake told him about the attempted murder of himself and Abe, and asked the deputy to put the three prisoners in jail until Sheriff Cassidy returned. Ellison walked to the window and looked at the prisoners outside.

'That's Raven,' he said, 'with Porter and Morse. They stay in town for a spell quite regular. We're pretty sure they work as hired killers, but there ain't never been enough evidence to charge them. Not until now, that is. I'll put them in one of the cells at the back.'

When this had been done Ellison told Jake and Abe that a stagecoach driver who had travelled on the coach from Cheyenne during the night was absolutely certain that there had been no bank robbery in Cheyenne on the morning of the previous day. He had been in the bank himself in the afternoon.

'I tried to telegraph the sheriff in Cheyenne, but the line is down,' said Ellison. 'There's a repair party out now, looking for the break. I'm sure the message we got was a fake. A couple of hours ago I sent out a fast rider to find Sheriff Cassidy to tell him so.'

'What Abe and me are figuring to do now,' said Jake, 'is ride out to Garner's claim and see what he has to say about leading us into a trap. If it's clear he's guilty, we'll bring him back here. Is that all right with you?'

'Sure,' said Ellison. 'I'm hoping the sheriff'll be back by tomorrow.'

Bannister was just coming out of his saloon when he was startled to see Jake and Abe leading their prisoners to the sheriff's office. Apprehensive, he joined the small group which had collected, and watched as the prisoners were taken inside. Then he hurried back into the saloon, and went to see Peary and his men. He told them what he had seen.

'I reckon it's time for you to leave Denver,' he said.

'You're right,' said Peary, and within the next twenty minutes they had left the saloon, picked up their horses from a small stable behind it, and had ridden, unobserved, behind the buildings, and out of town.

When Jake and Abe reached Garner's claim he was inside the small shack he had built, taking a meal. He heard them ride up and stepped outside. His jaw dropped as he saw the two men he believed to be dead. With rising panic he wondered what had happened to Raven and his men. Jake and Abe dismounted, keeping a close watch on the miner.

'Guess you're surprised to see us, Garner,' said Jake. 'That trap you led us into didn't work. That story you told us about the Peary gang riding through the ridge over there was a pack of lies. Raven and the others are in jail in Denver. It's clear that you were helping Raven in his plan to kill me and my partner, and you'll go to jail for that. But we want to know who hired Raven to kill us, and who put you in contact with Raven. Give us that information, and we'll ask the sheriff to put in a word for you with the judge.'

Garner licked his lips. He dreaded the thought of another long spell in prison. He told them how Bannister had arranged the meeting between himself and Raven, at which he agreed to pass false information to Jake. But he insisted that he was not told who had hired Raven, and he had no idea where the Peary gang was.

Garner was taken into Denver and handed over to Ellison. After hearing from Jake what they had learnt from the miner the deputy put Garner in a cell well away from that occupied by Raven and his men. Then Jake asked Ellison what he knew about Bannister.

'He don't give us no real trouble,' the deputy replied, 'though some folks say he runs a crooked game now and then. But that's never been proved.'

'We know for sure,' said Abe, 'that the Peary gang rode into Denver from Wyoming. Is there any chance they might be hiding in Bannister's place?'

'He doesn't run a hotel in there,' the deputy replied, 'but I think he has some rooms above the saloon. What he uses them for, I don't know.'

'But where would the gang put their horses?' asked Jake. 'They couldn't leave them at the livery stable.'

'Bannister keeps his own horse in a stable he built behind the saloon,' said Ellison. 'Maybe there's room for a few more in there.'

'What I'll do,' said Abe, 'is take a look round the back of the saloon, and see if I can spot any tracks made by the same horses we followed here from Wyoming. I won't be long.'

Abe returned twenty minutes later.

'We're in luck,' he said. 'The three horses we followed here left through the gate in the fence at the back of the saloon not more than a few hours ago, probably just after we brought Raven and his men in. They were ridden out of town, behind the buildings. I reckon I can follow them if we don't leave it too long.'

'Well,' said Jake, 'that pretty well proves that Bannister has been harbouring criminals. And he must have people in the saloon tending to them. It shouldn't be hard to get them to talk.

'It'll be dark soon,' he went on. 'In the morning we'll start following those tracks. We'll both sign a statement for the sheriff about Raven and his men trying to murder us, with Garner's help. And when you tell him about Bannister, I guess he'll want to take him in.'

'I think I'll go and have a word with him right now,' said the deputy. 'Maybe you'd like to come along?'

'All right,' said Jake. 'Abe'll stay in here to guard the prisoners while we're gone.'

But when they reached the saloon, they found that Bannister was not there, and nobody knew where he had gone. He had, in fact, heard of Garner's arrest, and had seen Abe looking round outside the rear of the saloon. As soon as Abe had disappeared, Bannister had hurriedly emptied the contents of his safe into a canvas bag which he tied on his horse, before riding, unobserved, out of town.

TEN

The following morning, after checking that Sheriff Cassidy had not yet returned, Jake and Abe followed the horse tracks of the Peary gang out of town towards the south. For several miles they ran parallel to the right bank of the South Platte River, then disappeared in the shallows. In an attempt to foil any pursuit, the gang had ridden in the water downstream, towards Denver, for over a mile. They had then crossed the river, and had ridden up the left bank, attempting to remove any signs that they had left the river at that point.

But they had not reckoned with Abe's tracking skills. Although the ruse delayed the pursuit for over an hour, he found the place where they had left the river and headed south-west, angling towards the distant peaks of the Rocky Mountain Range. Abe followed the tracks for fifteen miles, noting that no further efforts had been made to hide them.

'I reckon they're heading for a hideout some-where,' said Abe. 'Maybe not far from here. We'd best keep a lookout. Don't want them to know that we're on their trail.'

Ahead of them they could see the entrance to a narrow canyon, towards which the tracks were heading. They stopped, and Jake, using his field glasses, carefully inspected the canyon. He saw no sign of the gang, and it looked an unlikely place for a hideout. Following the tracks, they rode up to the canyon, and through it. They stopped near the exit, and dismounted. Jake moved forward and, through his field glasses, he surveyed the scene ahead.

He was looking over a flat area of ground, in the centre of which, slightly to his left, was an isolated, flat-topped hill with steep sides except at one point, facing west, where a gentle slope ran up from the plain to the top. It looked as though it would be possible to lead a horse up this slope, towards the foot of which the horse tracks leaving the canyon appeared to be heading.

Jake trained his glasses on the top of the hill, and slowly inspected the whole area. There was no sign of a lookout. Then, just as he was about to hand the glasses to Abe, he caught sight of a man who appeared briefly from behind a boulder, standing on top of the hill, then disappeared from view. Jake turned to Abe.

'I've just seen a man on top of the hill, Abe,' he said. 'Probably a lookout. I'm sure he's one of the men we're after. I need to work on a plan to get up there without getting shot. But *you've* finished the job I hired you to do. You've found them for me. If you want to leave now, that's all right with me.'

'I can't do that,' said Abe, 'not when things are starting to get exciting. I figure to stay with you till the job is done.'

'All right,' said Jake. 'I've got to say I feel a whole lot better with you along. I reckon we need to take a look at the far side of that hill before we decide what to do next.'

They rode back through the canyon, and half-circled the hill at a distance, keeping out of sight of the lookout. Then they approached it again, and took cover behind a large rocky outcrop. Once again, Jake observed the top of the hill through his field glasses. He noticed a small dark area on the side of the hill, near to the top. It looked like the entrance to a cave. As he was studying it a man came out and walked along a narrow ledge which ran for some distance to meet the gentle slope leading to the plain below. Here the man turned and walked up the slope to the top, then disappeared from view. A few minutes later another man appeared at the top, proceeded to the cave, and disappeared inside.

'Jus' saw two of them,' said Jake. 'It looked like

the lookout was being relieved.'

He closely examined the side of the hill through his glasses.

'Before I got married, Abe,' he said, 'I lived in the mountains for a spell, and I did some mountain climbing. During the night they'll be guarding the easy way up, but I can see a place where I reckon I could climb up the steep side in the dark. They'll have a night guard out watching the easy route to the top. What I'll do is climb up to the top after dark and take care of the night guard so we can surprise the other two in the cave. But I could do with some help to distract the guard, to make sure I can put him out of action before he raises the alarm.'

'And how do we do that?' asked Abe.

'I'm expecting,' Jake replied, 'that the night guard will be positioned where the ledge from the cave meets the path coming up from the plain. When I reach the top I'll keep well away from the guard, and give you a call to let you know I've reached the top. I'm expecting you'll be well up the slope by then, but out of sight of the guard.'

'What sort of a call?' asked Abe.

'A coyote is what I had in mind,' said Jake.

'Let's go round to the back of this outcrop,' said Abe, 'and you can give me a sample of what I'm going to hear.'

They moved round the outcrop, and Jake gave

his impression of the call of a coyote, and repeated it several times.

Abe winced. 'The Indians do it a lot better,' he said, 'but maybe that's as well. I'll know the calls are coming from you. What do I do when I hear them?'

'I want you to wait a few minutes, then sing one of your favourite cowboy songs,' said Jake, 'just loud enough for the guard to hear. I figure that when he hears the sound of your voice, all his attention is going to be fixed on you. That's when I creep up behind him and stun him with a blow on the head from the barrel of my pistol. Then I'll call you up, and we can sneak into the cave and capture the other two.'

'Sounds like it could work,' said Abe. 'My favourite song is "The Streets of Laredo". You reckon that would do?'

'Couldn't be better,' said Jake, and they settled down to wait for the start of the night operation.

It was half an hour past midnight when they set off. Each of them was carrying a six-gun and a coil of rope. Jake headed for the point at the foot of the hill from which he had decided to climb upwards. Abe headed for the foot of the gentle slope leading to the top.

Once Jake started climbing he realized it was not going to be as easy as he had expected. The slope was quite steep, and in the darkness handholds and footholds were difficult to find. Progress was slow. But he persisted until, about two thirds of the way to the top, he came to a section where the rock face was almost sheer. He climbed up this for several feet until, in the darkness, he could see no way of climbing any further. He decided that he had no option but to return to the bottom.

But when he tried to do this it was so dark that he could not see the necessary footholds, and the realization dawned on him that if he wished to avoid a possibly fatal fall he would have to stay where he was until there was enough light to make a safe descent possible. The two footholds he had were quite secure, and he was able to lean very slightly up against the wall, but the prospect of remaining in his present position until dawn was a daunting one.

It was a night which seemed without end, and which he would never forget. He spent the rest of it pressed up against the wall. His legs were aching, and he was conscious that the slightest relaxation could send him plummeting to his death below. As soon as there was enough light he started to climb down. He could not be seen from the entrance to the cave, which was some distance away. The danger was that if a lookout on top of the hill above Jake happened to look down over the edge, he was bound to see him. Slowly, he worked his way down, fearing discovery at any moment. But he reached the foot of the slope without being seen, and took refuge under a slight overhang nearby, where he was concealed from the outlaws above.

He decided that he had no option but to stay where he was until nightfall. He was almost bound to be seen by one of the gang if he crossed the plain, in daylight, to the outcrop where he and Abe had been hiding. He wondered what Abe had done when he had heard no signal from above. He settled down to await the time when he could return to the outcrop.

When Abe reached the foot of the narrow path leading to the top of the hill he started on a slow climb which took him to a point well up the slope, but out of sight of the guard above. On either side of the path the ground sloped downwards. He decided to wait there until he heard the signal from Jake.

He could see the outline of a small boulder standing at the edge of the path. He walked up to it, turned, and sat down on it. But when his full weight came down on the boulder, the ground underneath it suddenly gave way, and he and the boulder fell down the slope at the side of the path, ending up at the bottom. Abe was struck once by the boulder, at the beginning of the fall. The blow was to his right leg, which was badly wrenched in the process. He had also suffered numerous bruises on his body. The sounds of the fall of Abe and the boulder down the slope were not loud enough to attract the attention of the distant guard.

Abe checked his injured leg. The damage was worse than he had thought. He could feel the break below the knee. Walking was impossible. He could be of no help to Jake that night. Nor could he return to the safety of the outcrop, unaided. All he could do was wait in the hope that Jake would come to his help.

In order that he would not be seen by the outlaws when daylight came, he painfully dragged himself into a patch of brush close by. Once inside, he tied his two legs tightly together with the rope he was carrying with him. Then he resigned himself to staying where he was for the rest of the night, during which he heard no signal from Jake. He too had to stay where he was for the following day.

As soon as night had fallen Jake left the place at the foot of the hill where he had remained in hiding all day, and walked back to the outcrop. Abe was not there. Jake's fear was that somehow Abe had been captured by the outlaws during the previous night. He decided to return to the hill, after taking some food and drink, to see if there was any chance of finding and rescuing Abe.

He walked on foot to the bottom of the path which Abe had followed up the hill, and started walking up it. He paused as he heard the call of a coyote, repeated several times. It was very similar to the sample call which he himself had rendered earlier at the outcrop. It seemed to be coming from below Jake, to his right.

Jake hesitated, then returned to the bottom of the hill, swung left, and walked along the foot of the slope leading up to the path. He halted as, once again, he heard the call of a coyote, repeated several times. The source was ahead of him, and quite close. He moved forward, and stopped at the edge of a patch of brush.

'Is that you, Abe?' he called. 'This is Jake.'

'It's me,' Abe replied. 'I'm in the brush. Got a busted leg. Can't move. I sure am glad you found me.'

Jake made his way into the brush, and bent down over Abe to check his injury. Then he lifted him upright and slung him over his shoulder.

'First thing is to get you back to the outcrop,' he said. 'We'll talk after that.'

Staggering under Abe's weight, Jake moved slowly back to the outcrop, where he laid his part-ner on the ground, removed the rope from around his legs, and closely examined the injury.

'Looks like a clean break, Abe,' he said, 'but I need to get you to a doctor, if it's going to heal right. What's the nearest town, d'you reckon?'

'That would be Silver Spring,' said Abe. 'Maybe twelve miles south.'

'Right,' said Jake. 'We'll go there. But first, I'll get you some food and drink. Then I'm riding back to that grove of trees we passed not far from here. I'll cut some pieces of timber I can use to make splints and a travois. The worst thing you could do is ride a horse with that leg. We'll talk more when I get back.'

When Jake returned he started work on the fashioning of the splints and travois. While engaged on this he told Abe of his own bad luck in failing to reach the top of the hill, and Abe recounted his own unfortunate experience of falling down the slope.

'We were both just plumb out of luck,' he said, and went on to ask Jake what he intended to do after reaching Silver Spring.

'When we've seen the doctor, and got you fixed up,' said Jake, 'I'll leave you to rest up there for a spell, and I'll come back to the outcrop. I'll figure out some way of capturing those three before they decide to move on.'

'I'm mighty sorry this has happened,' said Abe. 'I was figuring on staying with you till the job was finished.'

After the splints had been fitted to Abe's leg they waited until daybreak. Then Abe was helped on to the travois, which was being pulled by his own horse. They reached Silver Spring before noon, and soon found the house of Doc Trimble. He answered Jake's knock, and helped him to bring Abe inside. He was a short man, brisk and cheerful. He complimented Jake on the splints, and when they had come off he examined the leg.

'This should heal up fine,' he said. 'I'll put some of my own splints on, and lend you a pair of crutches. Take it easy, and you'll be walking normal again before long. If you like you can stay here for a spell. I've got plenty of room.'

They thanked the doctor, and Jake paid him for Abe's treatment and accommodation. Then he had a few words with Abe before he left.

'I'm obliged to you, Abe,' he said, 'for finding the Peary gang for me. I'd like to stay here with you till you're fit, but that could mean me losing contact with the gang.'

He handed Abe the amount required to cover his hire until he got back to Cheyenne. He promised to call on him there when he had completed his mission.

ELEVEN

When Jake reached the outcrop he resumed the watch which he and Abe had been keeping over the outlaws, hideout during the daytime. He had barely settled down to do this when he saw a man leading a horse down from the top of the hill. The other two outlaws appeared from inside the cave, and watched him go. Then they walked back inside. Jake took a look through his field glasses at the man walking the horse. It was Donovan.

On reaching the bottom of the hill, the outlaw mounted his horse and rode off in a direction which would take him fairly close to the outcrop. Jake moved round it with his horse to a position which would not be visible to Donovan as he passed. Observing the rider a few minutes later, Jake could see that he was riding in the direction of Silver Spring, and the thought occurred to him that Donovan was going for supplies to bring back to the hideout.

Jake decided to follow him to Silver Spring, and capture him there. If he managed this he would then have only two outlaws left to deal with. He followed Donovan, taking care that the outlaw did not become aware of his presence. When his hunch proved correct, and he saw Donovan ride into Silver Spring, he waited a short while, then rode up to the outskirts, dismounted, and walked into town, leaving his horse behind. He soon saw Donovan's horse, standing at the hitching rail outside the general store. As he approached the store along the boardwalk the door opened and Donovan came out, carrying a sack of provisions. He glanced at Jake, dropped the sack, and made a fast draw with his right hand. But Jake's draw was quicker, and he had the advantage of surprise. He had time to target, with his Peacemaker, Donovan's right arm before the outlaw had triggered his six-gun. Donovan's gun fell to the boardwalk, and he stood holding his injured arm, and staring at Jake.

The sound of the shot drew several people out on to the street, including Doc Trimble, who walked up to Jake.

'Is this one of the outlaws you were telling me about?' he asked.

'That's right,' replied Jake. 'His name is Donovan. I aim to go after the other two as soon as I can. After you've tended to this man's arm, d'you think he can be held in town here for the law to pick up?'

'I can see to that,' said Trimble. 'I know several men in town who'll be willing to take turns guarding him. And I'll get a message to the sheriff at Pueblo to have him picked up.'

'I'm obliged,' said Jake. 'Sheriff Grant in Pueblo knows I'm chasing the gang. I'll take Donovan to your house, and have a word with Abe.'

While Donovan's wound was being tended to, Jake told Abe, in the next room, of the capture of Donovan, who would be held in town till the law picked him up.

'That's good news,' said Abe. I'll take a turn at guarding him. Maybe my leg's busted, but I can still handle a gun. You'll be going back for the other two?'

'That's right,' said Jake. 'Right now. It'll be dark before I get there, and they'll be expecting Donovan about the same time. So I'll take Donovan's place. In the dark there's a good chance of me getting away with it long enough to get the better of them. I think I'll borrow that sugar-loaf sombrero that Donovan wears. It could help in the dark.'

He picked up the sombrero and rode out of town, back to the outlaws' hideout, arriving there after nightfall. He dismounted at the foot of the path leading to the top of the hill. Then, leaving his horse at the bottom, he walked up the path, and stopped within hailing distance of the top of the slope.

'This is Donovan,' he called. 'I'm coming up.'

He waited for a response, but none came. He repeated the call several times, but there was still no reply, and no sound of any kind. He drew his Peacemaker, and walked slowly up the path, straining his eyes to see what lay ahead. Eventually, without seeing or hearing any sign of a guard, he reached the point where the path met the ledge leading to the cave. Maybe, he thought, Peary and Barton had decided a night guard was not necessary.

Silently, he moved along the ledge towards the cave, and paused just before reaching the entrance. He could hear no sounds inside. Still holding his six-gun, he slipped into the cave, keeping hard up against the side of the entrance. Having no idea how big it was, he moved forward a few paces, then stopped to listen. He could see nothing in the pitch blackness of the cave's interior. During the next few minutes no sound, except for his own breathing, broke the silence. Cautiously, he started to move around, and soon came to the conclusion that the cave was quite small, and that it was empty. He confirmed this by lighting matches, and it soon became evident that Peary and Barton had vacated it, taking their belongings, after Donovan's departure for Silver Spring.

Jake left the cave, and went to the top of the hill. He soon found the hollow, now empty, where the horses had been kept. He returned to the cave and stayed there until daybreak, when he descended the hill to his horse and made an attempt to follow the tracks left by Peary and Barton. He succeeded in doing this for a couple of miles, during which the tracks were heading a little east of south. He wondered whether Donovan had intended to rejoin the others somewhere, after calling at Silver Spring for supplies.

But then, wishing that Abe was with him, he lost the tracks on a stretch of hard ground, and was unable to pick them up again. He was not far from Silver Spring, and decided to call in to see Abe before considering his next move. When he arrived there he went to the doctor's house and told Trimble and Abe about Peary and Barton leaving the hideout.

'Has Donovan been talking at all?' he asked. 'He'll know where the other two have gone.'

'Nary a word,' said Abe. 'He's tight as a clam. I don't think you'll get anything out of him.'

'I sure wish I knew where they were heading,' said Jake. 'Did you find anything interesting in Donovan's pockets?'

'I've got the contents in a drawer here,' said the

doctor. 'Didn't look at them close. Was aiming to hand them over to whoever comes to pick him up.'

'Let's take a look at them,' said Jake. Trimble took a large envelope out of a drawer and emptied the contents on a table. Jake looked down at them. One item which caught his attention was a crumpled folded sheet of paper. He picked it up, unfolded it, and examined it closely. The top of the sheet was marked NORTH. Just below this was a cross marked EAGLE BLUFF. From this cross, a line running east was marked RIVER. There was a further cross at the side of the river, and the distance between this cross and Eagle Bluff was shown as 11 MILES.

'This is interesting,' said Jake, handing the sheet of paper to Abe. 'I wonder whether Donovan was aiming to meet up with the others at the place by the river marked with a cross? Maybe these directions were given to him by Peary or Barton. But where the devil is Eagle Bluff? I've never heard of it.'

Abe studied the paper, and cast his mind back over his many years of Army service, conjuring up memories of the areas in which he had operated.

'I'm sure I've seen this Eagle Bluff,' he said, 'but that was a long time ago. I'm trying to remember just where it's located. Give me a minute or two. Maybe it'll come back to me.'

He closed his eyes, wrinkled his brow, and sat

motionless for a short while. Then his eyes flicked open.

'Got it!' he shouted. 'It's twelve years since I saw Eagle Bluff. There may be others with the same name, but the one I saw did have a river running close by it in an easterly direction. It's in the northern part of the Texas Panhandle, not far from the border with New Mexico Territory.'

'That lines up with the direction Peary and Barton were heading,' said Jake. 'I think I'll take a chance, and ride down there to see if there's any sign of them. I'll start off now and camp out overnight.'

Jake left Silver Spring, after getting more information from Abe about the location of Eagle Bluff. After a long ride without incident he arrived there about noon, recognizing the bluff by its distinctive shape, as described to him by Abe. He rode east along the south bank of the narrow river running past the bluff. On reaching a point which he estimated as being about ten miles from the bluff he caught sight of a cabin, well ahead of him, standing a little way from the south bank of the river.

He stopped and dismounted, then looked at the cabin through his field glasses. It was standing on a flat area of ground, well away from all the main trails in the area. He could see no sign of horses nearby. Nor was there any indication that people were staying there. The thought occurred to him that if this was indeed the hideout, then Peary and Barton might have broken their journey some-where, and would be turning up later.

He watched the cabin for another fifteen minutes, then rode on towards it, keeping it under close observation, and ready to respond to any fire. But none came, and he dismounted outside the door, holding his six-gun. The cabin had clearly stood there for a long time, and had an aban-doned look about it. He walked inside, and saw no indications that it had been occupied recently. He decided to find a place from which he could keep the cabin under observation, using his field glasses.

He looked round. Towards the south was an area of hilly ground which looked worth investi-gating. He rode up to it and could see, ahead of him, the entrance to a narrow ravine in which he and his horse could hide. From the top of it the cabin would be clearly visible. He rode up to the entrance, then along the floor of the ravine. He rounded a slight bend, and came to a sudden halt.

In front of him he was startled to see an almost exact replica of Hank Logan, who had rescued him from the mine tunnel. A mule and a burro stood close by. Then Jake remembered Hank telling him he had a twin brother, Luke, a wander-ing prospector like himself.

'You must be Luke Logan,' said Jake. 'Your

brother Hank helped me out of some trouble not long ago. You sure favour him.'

Luke laid down the shotgun he was holding. 'How's Hank doing?' he asked. 'I ain't seen him for quite a spell.'

Quickly, Jake gave him a full account of recent events, including the murder of Hank. Luke was visibly shocked. He sat on the ground for a while, without speaking. Then he looked up at Jake.

'I'd sure like to help you catch those outlaws that murdered Hank,' he said.

'I can do with all the help I can get,' said Jake, 'but it would be a risky business for you. You know that killing means nothing to them. You sure you want to get mixed up in this?'

'I know I ain't as spry as I used to be,' said Luke, 'but I can still handle a knife and a gun. I'd like to help.'

'All right,' said Jake. 'What I'm going to do now is ride a mile or two further along the river to see if there's any other possible hideout for them. Then I'll come back here.'

He returned, an hour and a half later, to tell Luke that his search had proved negative.

'What I aim to do for the next few days; he said, 'is stay here and watch the cabin.'

'That's something I *can* help you with,' said Luke.

It was nine o'clock the following morning when

Luke called down to Jake that he could see four riders approaching the cabin along the bank of the river. Jake joined him, and Luke handed him the field glasses. The four riders stopped outside the cabin, dismounted, and went inside.

'I see Peary and Barton,' said Jake, 'and a couple of other men I don't recognize. It looks like Peary has recruited two more men into the gang. So now we've got *four* men to deal with. Are you sure you still want to hang around here, Luke?'

'I'm sure,' said the prospector. 'You got some plan to cover the situation?'

'I'm working on it,' said Jake. 'I'm wondering if there's some way we can deal with them one at a time.'

Just after midday Jake was watching the cabin when he saw Barton come out and walk over to the horses, on a picket line a little way south of the cabin. He mounted one of the horses and started riding along a faint trail, in a direction which would take him past the ravine and about a quarter of a mile clear of it. Jake had a sudden thought. He hurried down to Luke. He told him that Barton was riding off, and that he was going to try and intercept him. He asked Luke for the loan of his shotgun, mounted his horse, and rode out of the ravine, still out of sight of Barton. He headed fast for a large rocky outcrop adjacent to the trail which the outlaw was following. He rode behind

151

the outcrop, out of sight of the approaching rider. He dismounted, and from cover he watched the progress of the oncoming outlaw.

Just as Barton was passing the outcrop Jake ran out in front of him, with his shotgun trained on the rider. The shocked Barton recognized Jake and, knowing the damage a shotgun blast could do at short range, he hurriedly reined in his horse. He sat staring at Jake, his arms half-raised.

'We're taking a short ride, Barton,' said Jake. 'You'll be in the lead. I'll tell you where to go. This shotgun will be aimed at your back all the time, and the trigger's cocked. So I wouldn't do anything foolish, if I were you.'

Jake told Barton to turn round. Then he mounted his own horse, and directed the outlaw to the ravine, where Luke saw them coming. Relieved that Jake had successfully completed his mission, he grinned as they rode up to him and stopped.

'Number one,' he said. 'Three to go.'

'That's right,' said Jake. 'If you'll give me a hand, we'll tie this one up for the time being.'

When the outlaw had been securely tied he was left lying on the ground. Luke and Jake moved away from him.

'I've been wondering where Barton was going,' said Jake. 'You can see he has his bedroll with him, so it looks like he wasn't expecting to be back at the cabin tonight. Let's watch the cabin till dark, then think up a plan to capture the others.'

As darkness was falling Jake came down from the observation point to join Luke below.

'I've noticed, Luke,' he said, 'that they have a guard posted outside the cabin all the time, and the guard is changed every four hours, at four, eight and twelve. I expect it's the same during the night. And when the time comes for a change, the guard on duty opens the cabin door, just long enough to call out to one of the men inside, who comes out a little later to relieve him. This delay between the time the relief guard is called, and the time he appears outside, is probably longer during the night. Maybe we can make use of it.'

They discussed for a while the plan which Jake had in mind. Luke reckoned it could work, and they decided to give it a try. They had a meal, gave Barton some food and drink, then each of them had three hours' sleep while the other guarded the prisoner. At three o'clock in the morning they made sure that Barton would find it impossible to free himself, or move from the position where he was lying. Then they rode out of the ravine, Luke on Barton's horse, and proceeded towards the cabin through the darkness. They stopped outside the guard's view, and picketed the horses. They could just see the outlaws' horses, between them and the cabin. Then, just after half past three Jake, who knew that the guard usually stood at the front of the cabin, circled round it and approached it cautiously from the rear.

For the next ten minutes, as he stood against the cabin wall, Jake heard the guard cough several times. Then he heard the door opening, and closing a minute or so later. He moved round the cabin towards the front wall, and threw a large stone which landed in front of Brand, the guard, but well away from him. Brand stiffened, and moved forward a couple of paces, staring straight ahead. Jake came up silently behind him, and pistol-whipped him with the long barrel of his .45 Peacemaker.

As an ex-lawman, Jake had a fair idea of the amount of force necessary to stun his victim for a short length of time. As Brand collapsed, Jake caught him, then dragged him as quickly as he could to the waiting Luke.

'Number two,' he said, hurriedly, 'and number three in a few minutes, if our luck holds out.'

Swiftly, they gagged and tied Brand, then Jake ran back to the cabin, wearing Brand's hat, and stood with his back to the door, a few paces from it.

He was just in time. The door opened behind him, and Carson, the relief guard, came out, leaving a lamp burning dimly inside. He closed the door behind him, then remarked on the chilliness

154

of the night air as he walked up to the shadowy figure in front of him. Jake turned round, and the unsuspecting Carson received the same treatment as that meted out to the man he thought he was relieving. Jake dragged him back to Luke, and he was quickly bound and gagged.

'That leaves Peary,' said Jake. 'These two I don't know. But they're probably outlaws, otherwise they wouldn't be here with Peary. I'm going for Peary. Wait here for me, Luke.'

Jake returned to the cabin, holding his six-gun. He opened the door slowly, and slid inside. The lamp was still burning dimly, but it gave sufficient light to show him that the cabin was empty. Peary must have left it during the short period since the capture of the relief guard.

Jake left the cabin, on the alert for any sign of the gang leader. He walked back to Luke, collecting the three outlaws' horses on the way. He gave Luke the bad news.

'Peary is somewhere out there,' he said, 'mad as hell, and armed, and wondering if he can turn the tables on us. But he's afoot, and he don't know how many of us there are. I reckon we should go back to the ravine with the prisoners and these three horses I've just picked up. When daylight comes I'll go after Peary. I expect he'll be around here somewhere. Meantime, let's both keep an eye out for him.'

They slung the two prisoners over the backs of two horses, and led them, with the third horse, to the ravine. They laid Carson and Brand on the ground, near Barton. Then Jake, holding his six-gun, and Luke, holding his shotgun, sat down between the horses and the prisoners, looking and listening for any sign of Peary.

'You sure he'll still be around at daybreak?' asked Luke.

'Knowing Peary, I'm sure he will,' Jake replied.

The remainder of the night passed without incident. At daybreak Jake had breakfast. Then he prepared to set out on a search for the gang leader, after each of the prisoners in turn had been freed for a short spell, and had been given food and drink.

'Keep that shotgun handy while I'm away, Luke,' he said. 'I'll get back as soon as I can.'

He rode down the ravine, round the slight bend, and past a patch of brush, head-high, standing at the foot of the wall of the ravine. As he was passing this he saw out of the corner of his eye the slightest of movements inside it. As he turned his mount, Peary burst out of the brush, firing at Jake. Simultaneously Jake fired at him. Peary's shot grazed Jake's right temple, but not deeply enough to knock him out. Jake's shot drilled into Peary's heart. The outlaw leader went down. The sound of gunfire brought Luke running to the scene. He found Jake leaning over the outlaw's body.

'It's Peary,' said Jake. 'He was hiding in the brush there. He's dead. Could have been me. I had a big slice of luck. This is the end of my chase, Luke. It sure has been a long one. I'm real obliged for your help. If you don't mind helping out just a bit longer, I aim to send a telegraph message to US Marshal Ryan in Amarillo. I'll tell him that Bart Peary is dead, and we're holding Barton and two other members of the gang prisoner.

'I'll tell him where we are, and ask him to have the prisoners picked up. D'you know where the nearest town is, Luke?'

'Probably one I passed through three days ago,' Luke replied. 'About three hours from here on a good horse. I remember seeing a telegraph office there.'

'If I write a message out, will you take it there while I guard the prisoners here?' asked Jake. 'You can use my horse. Tell the operator you want a quick reply, and wait for it. Then come back here.'

'I'll do that,' said Luke, 'and glad to. I'll be back as quick as I can.' He rode off shortly after, and returned after dark with a reply to the telegraph message. In it, Ryan said that two Texas Rangers with a jail wagon would pick up the prisoners three days later.

When the wagon arrived Jake rode back with it to Amarillo. Before parting from Luke he told him that he was aiming to buy a ranch in Wyoming, north of Cheyenne, and if Luke ever felt like settling down, and living on a small ranch, he'd be welcome there.

The trial of the three prisoners took place in Amarillo three days after their arrival there. Jake attended as a witness. All three were wanted for robbery and murder, and all were sentenced to death by hanging. The following morning Jake headed for Pueblo.

After arriving there he had a brief conversation with Sheriff Grant, then went in search of Billy. He found him at the laundry. The boy was obviously relieved and pleased to see him.

'I've finished the job, Billy,' he said. 'Now we can go to Wyoming to find a ranch we can run together.'

'Can we go soon?' asked Billy.

'We'll leave tomorrow,' Jake replied. 'We'll take the stagecoach to Cheyenne.'

When they reached Cheyenne Jake took Billy along to meet Abe, who had returned there, and whose leg was improving rapidly. Jake told him about Peary's death, and the capture of the others.

'Me and Billy here,' he went on, 'are aiming to run a cattle ranch in Wyoming, probably not far from here. I got the idea that you ain't too happy living alone here in Cheyenne, and maybe, when we've found a place that suits us, you'd like to come and live on the ranch with us?'

'This is the best offer I've had for a long time,' said Abe, 'and I'm going to grab it before you change your mind. But only on condition I'm allowed to pull my weight. I can still do a good day's work.'

'Agreed.' Jake smiled. 'You'll be in charge of tracking down any cows that have strayed off our range.'

Two months later Abe joined Jake and Billy on the spread which Jake had taken over, about seventy miles north of Cheyenne.

Billy attended school in a nearby town. The schoolteacher was an attractive widow, in her early thirties. In the course of time a friendship burgeoned between her and Jake. But that's another story.